BENNY AND ~~PENNY~~ IN
LIGHTS OUT!

A TOON BOOK BY
GEOFFREY HAYES

TOON BOOKS • NEW YORK

A JUNIOR LIBRARY GUILD SELECTION
KIRKUS BEST CONTINUING SERIES

Make sure to find all the Benny and Penny books:
Benny and Penny in Just Pretend
Benny and Penny in The Big No-No!, **A GEISEL AWARD WINNER!**
Benny and Penny in The Toy Breaker
Benny and Penny in Lost and Found
Benny and Penny in Lights Out!
Benny and Penny in How to Say Goodbye

For Pascual—a little night music!

Editorial Director: FRANÇOISE MOULY

Book Design: FRANÇOISE MOULY

GEOFFREY HAYES' artwork was drawn in colored pencil.

A TOON Book™ © 2012 Geoffrey Hayes & TOON Books, an imprint of RAW Junior, LLC, 27 Greene Street, New York, NY 10013. No part of this book may be used or reproduced in any manner whatsoever without written permission except in the case of brief quotations embodied in critical articles and reviews. TOON Graphics™, TOON Books®, LITTLE LIT® and TOON Into Reading!™ are trademarks of RAW Junior, LLC. All rights reserved. Library of Congress Cataloging-in-Publication Data: Hayes, Geoffrey. Benny and Penny in Lights out! : a TOON book / by Geoffrey Hayes.   p. cm.   Summary: At bedtime two mouse siblings take turns telling stories and calming night fears. hardcover ISBN 978-1-935179-20-7 1. Graphic novels. [1. Graphic novels. 2. Bedtime--Fiction. 3. Brothers and sisters--Fiction. 4. Mice--Fiction.] I. Title. II. Title: Lights out!   PZ7.7.H39Bc 2012 741.5'973--dc23   2011050927   All our books are Smyth Sewn (the highest library-quality binding available) and printed with soy-based inks on acid-free, woodfree paper harvested from responsible sources. Printed in China by C&C Offset Printing Co., Ltd. Distributed to the trade by Consortium Book Sales & Distribution, a division of Ingram Content Group; orders (866) 400-5351; ips@ingramcontent.com; www.cbsd.com.
ISBN 978-1-935179-20-7 (hardcover)   ISBN 978-1-943145-49-2 (paperback)
19 20 21 22 23 24 C&C 10 9 8 7 6 5 4 3
www.TOON-BOOKS.com

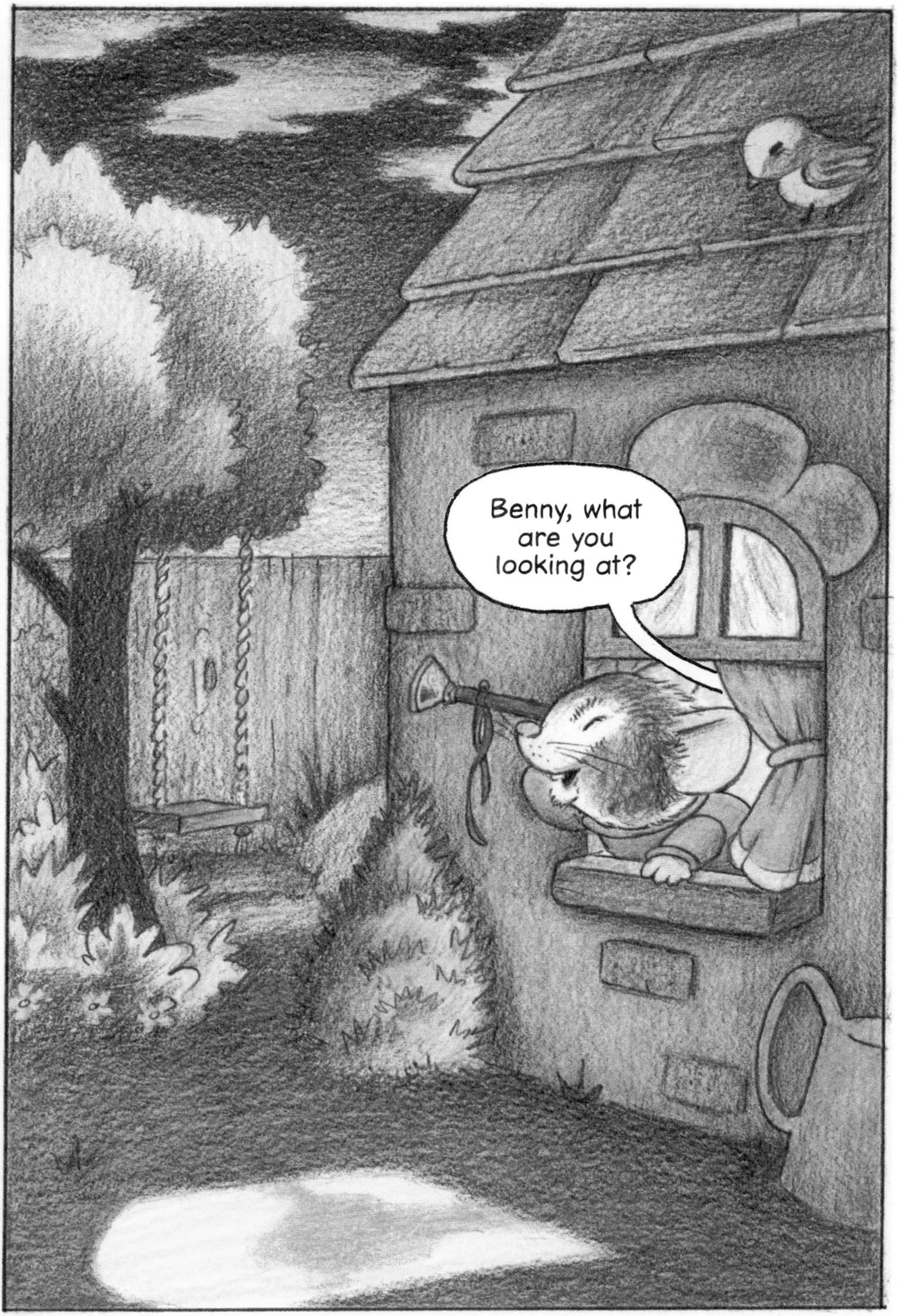
Benny, what are you looking at?

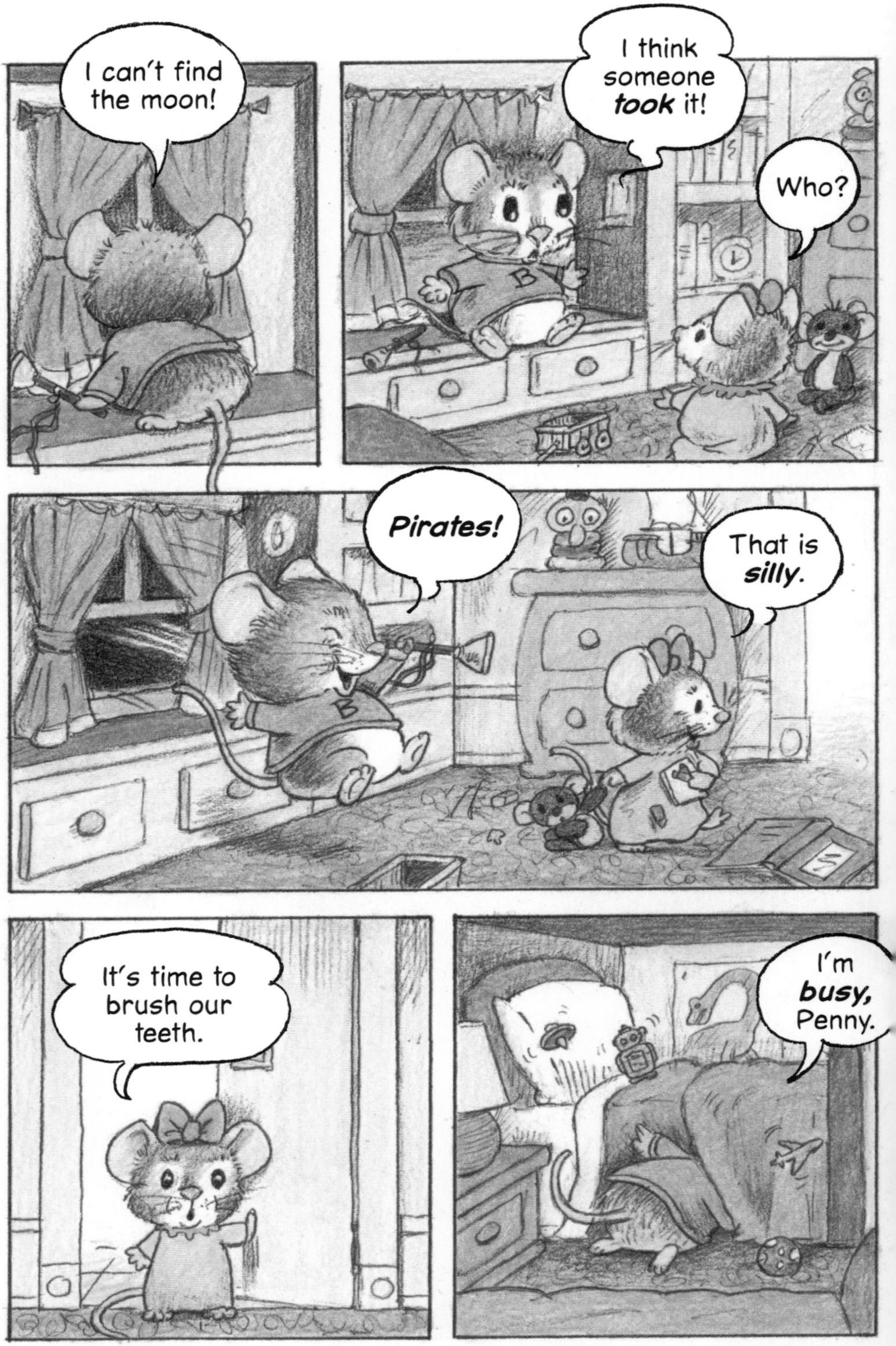

I can't find the moon!
I think someone ***took*** it!
Who?
Pirates!
That is ***silly***.
It's time to brush our teeth.
I'm ***busy,*** Penny.

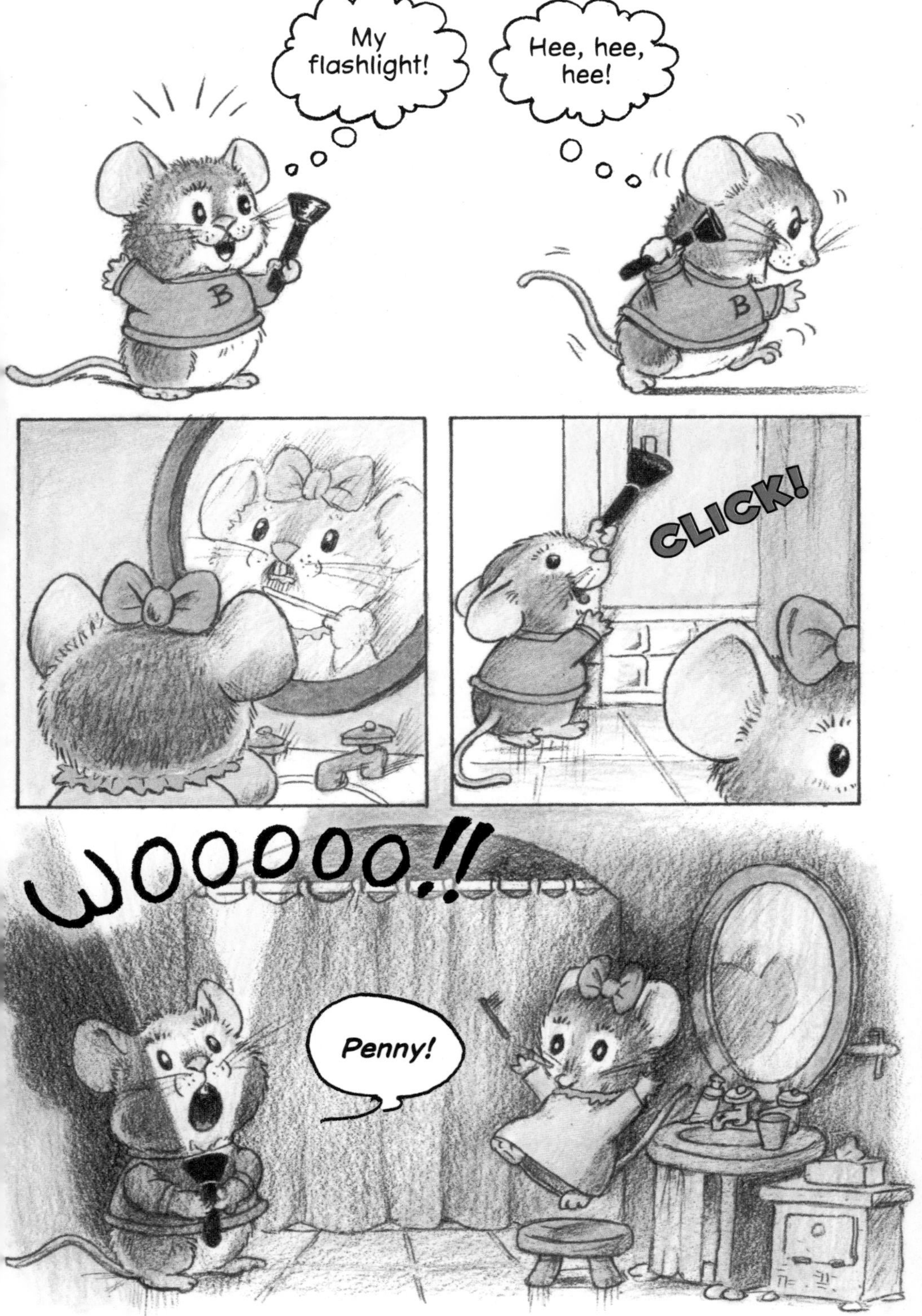
My flashlight!
Hee, hee, hee!
CLICK!
WOOOOO!!
Penny!

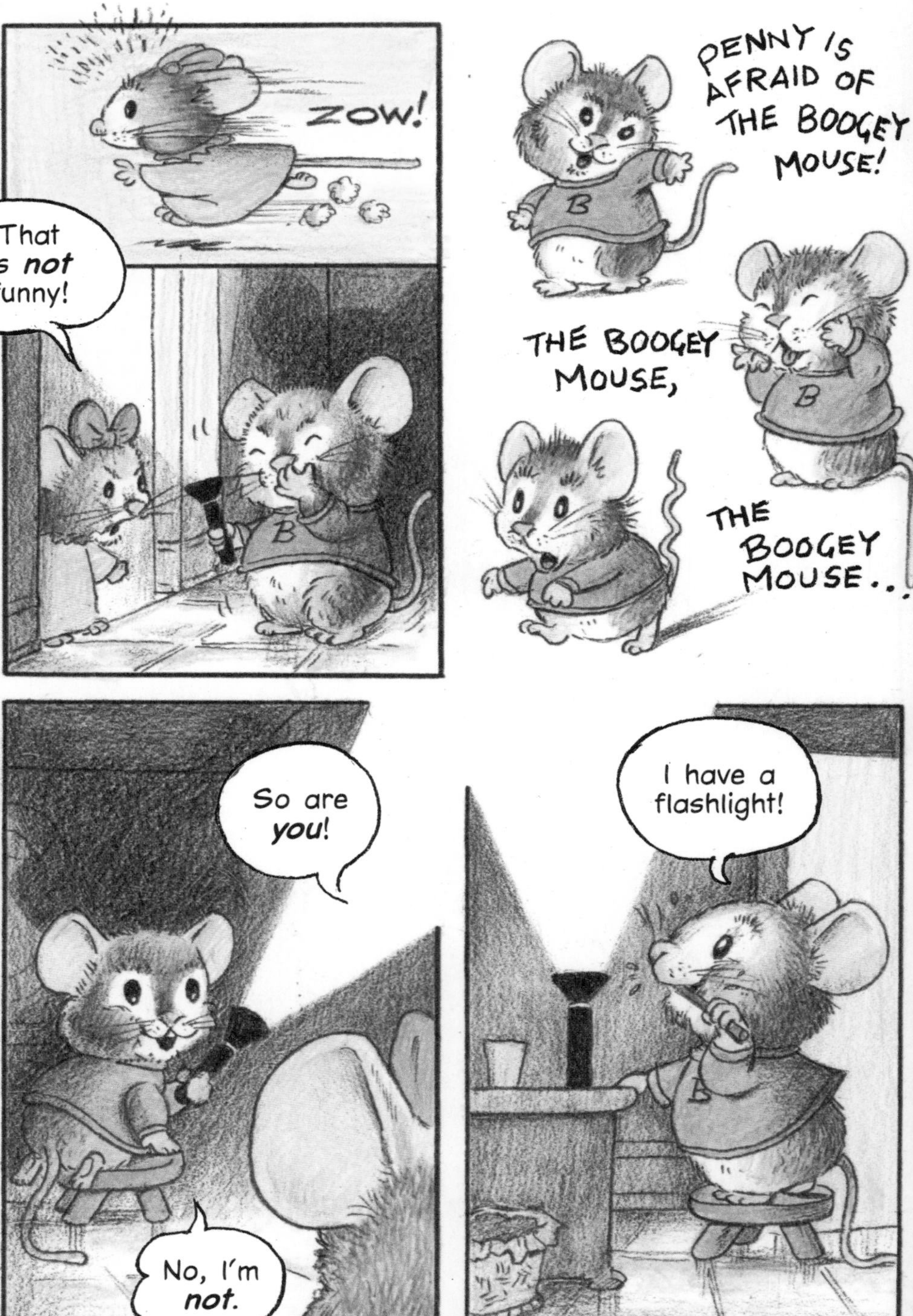

ZOW!
That is not funny!
PENNY IS AFRAID OF THE BOOGEY MOUSE!
THE BOOGEY MOUSE,
THE BOOGEY MOUSE...
So are you!
No, I'm not.
I have a flashlight!

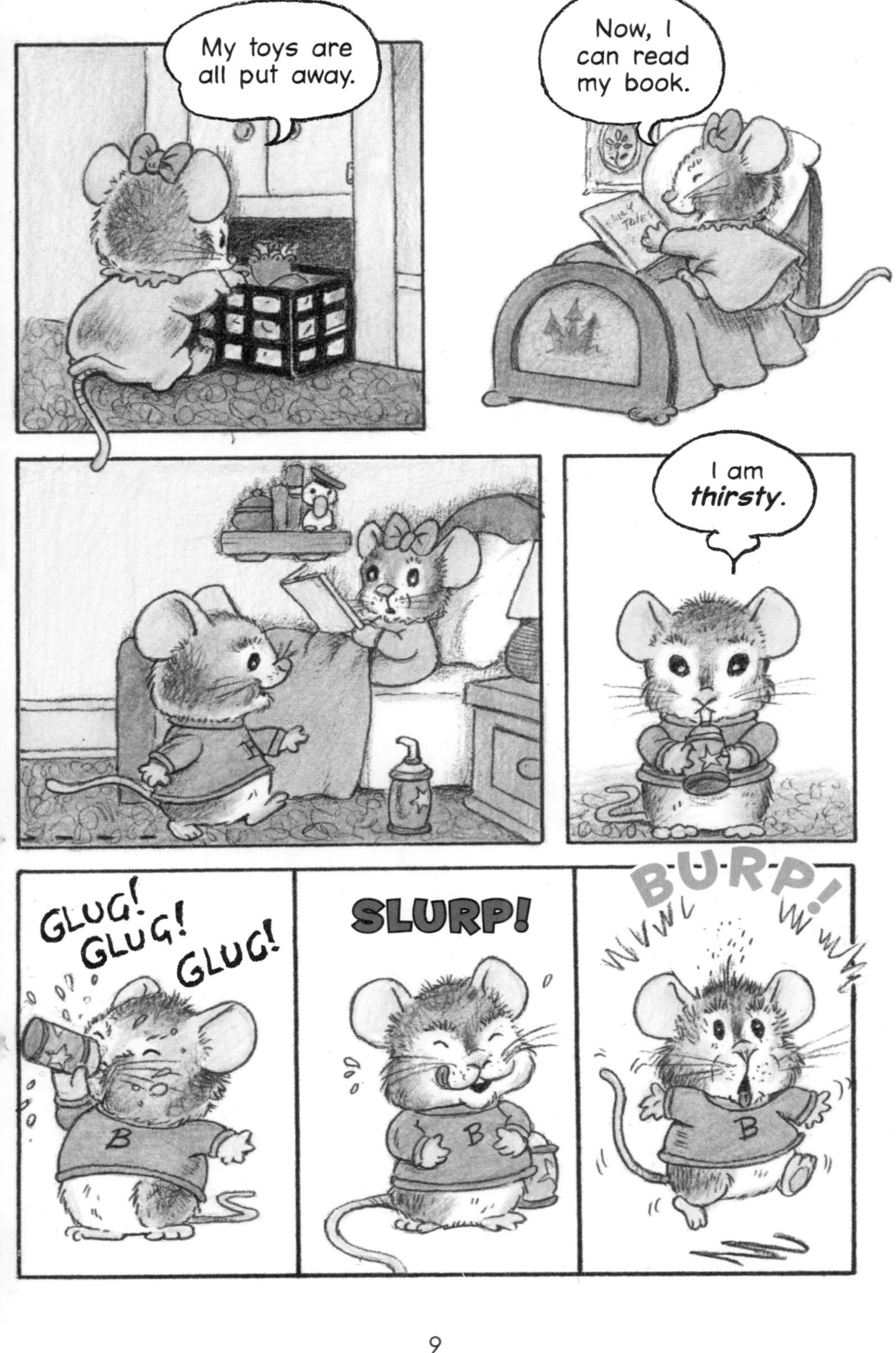

My toys are all put away.
Now, I can read my book.
I am *thirsty*.
GLUG! GLUG! GLUG!
SLURP!
BURP!

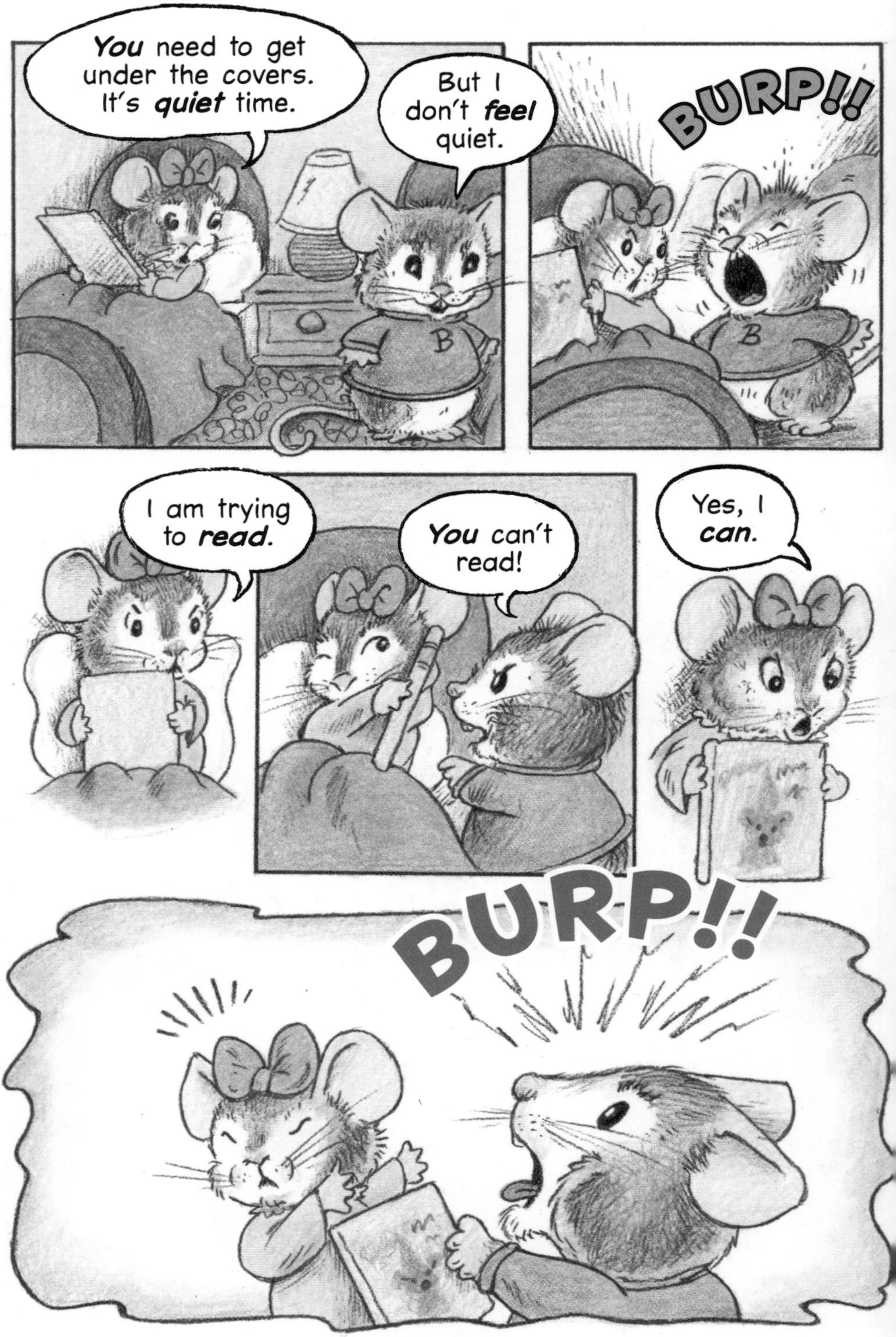
You need to get under the covers. It's ***quiet*** time.
But I don't ***feel*** quiet.
BURP!!
I am trying to ***read***.
You can't read!
Yes, I ***can***.
BURP!!

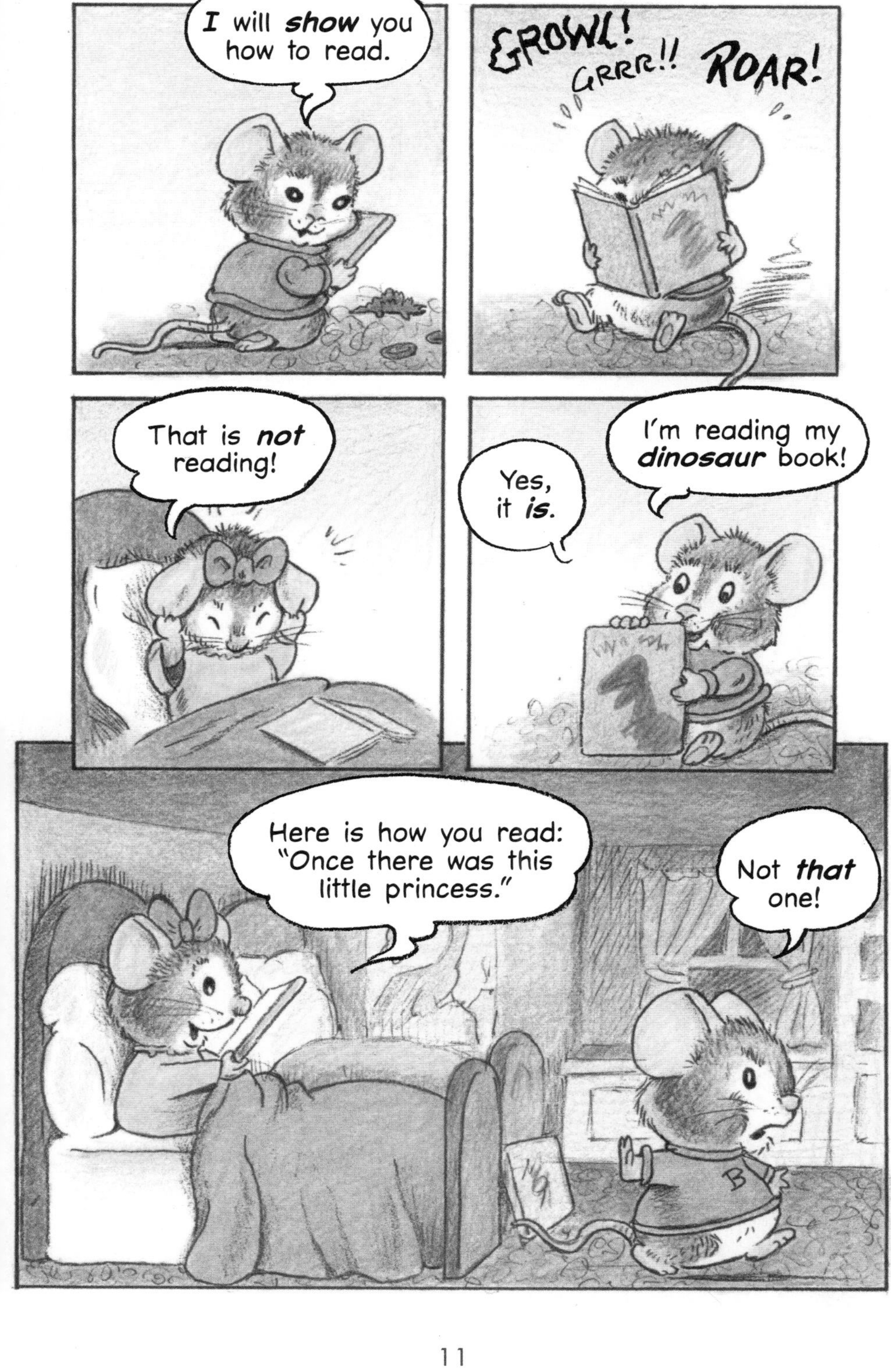

I will show you how to read.
GROWL!
GRRR!!
ROAR!
That is not reading!
Yes, it is.
I'm reading my dinosaur book!
Here is how you read: "Once there was this little princess."
Not that one!

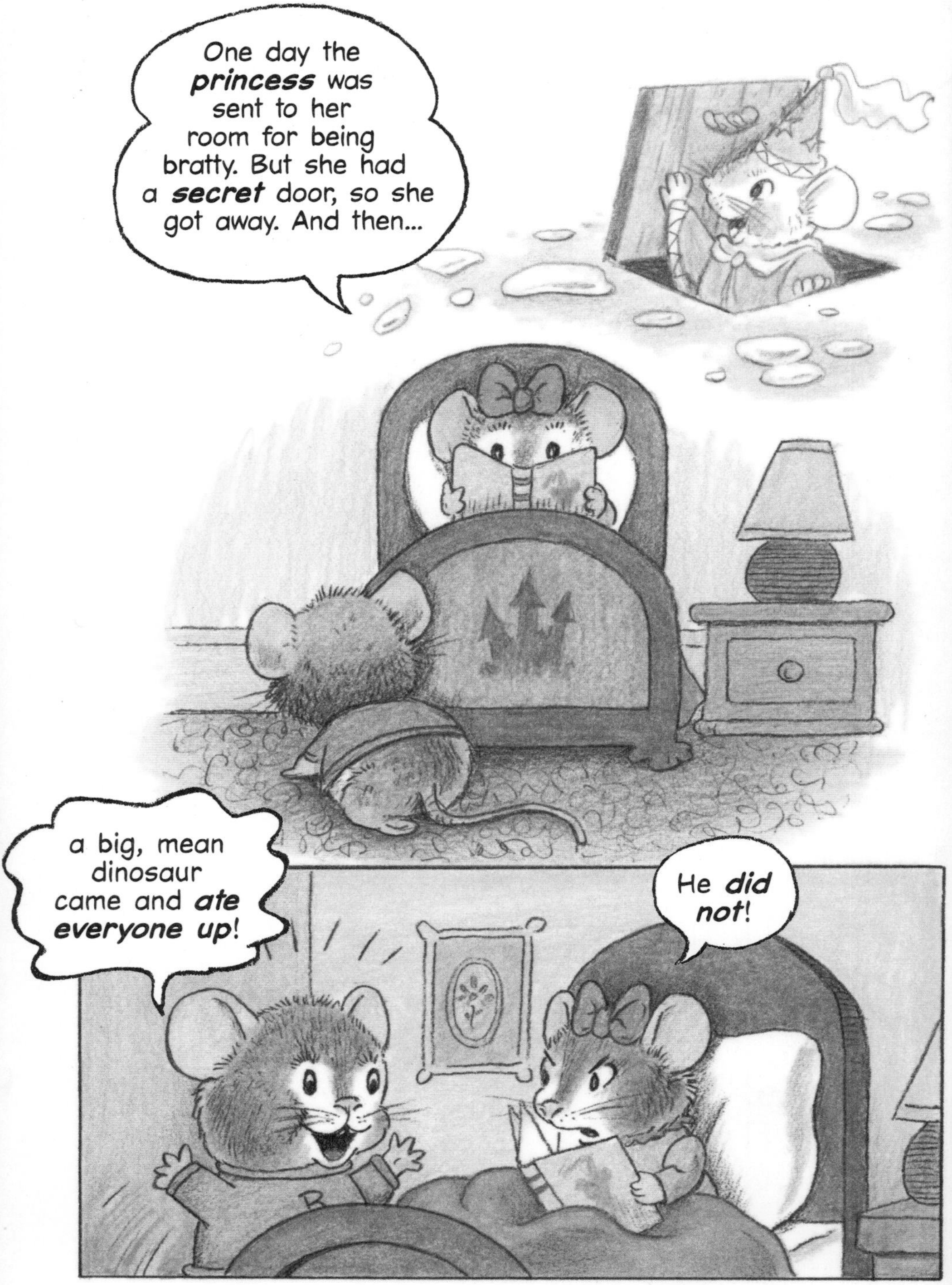
One day the ***princess*** was sent to her room for being bratty. But she had a ***secret*** door, so she got away. And then...
a big, mean dinosaur came and ***ate everyone up***!
He ***did not***!

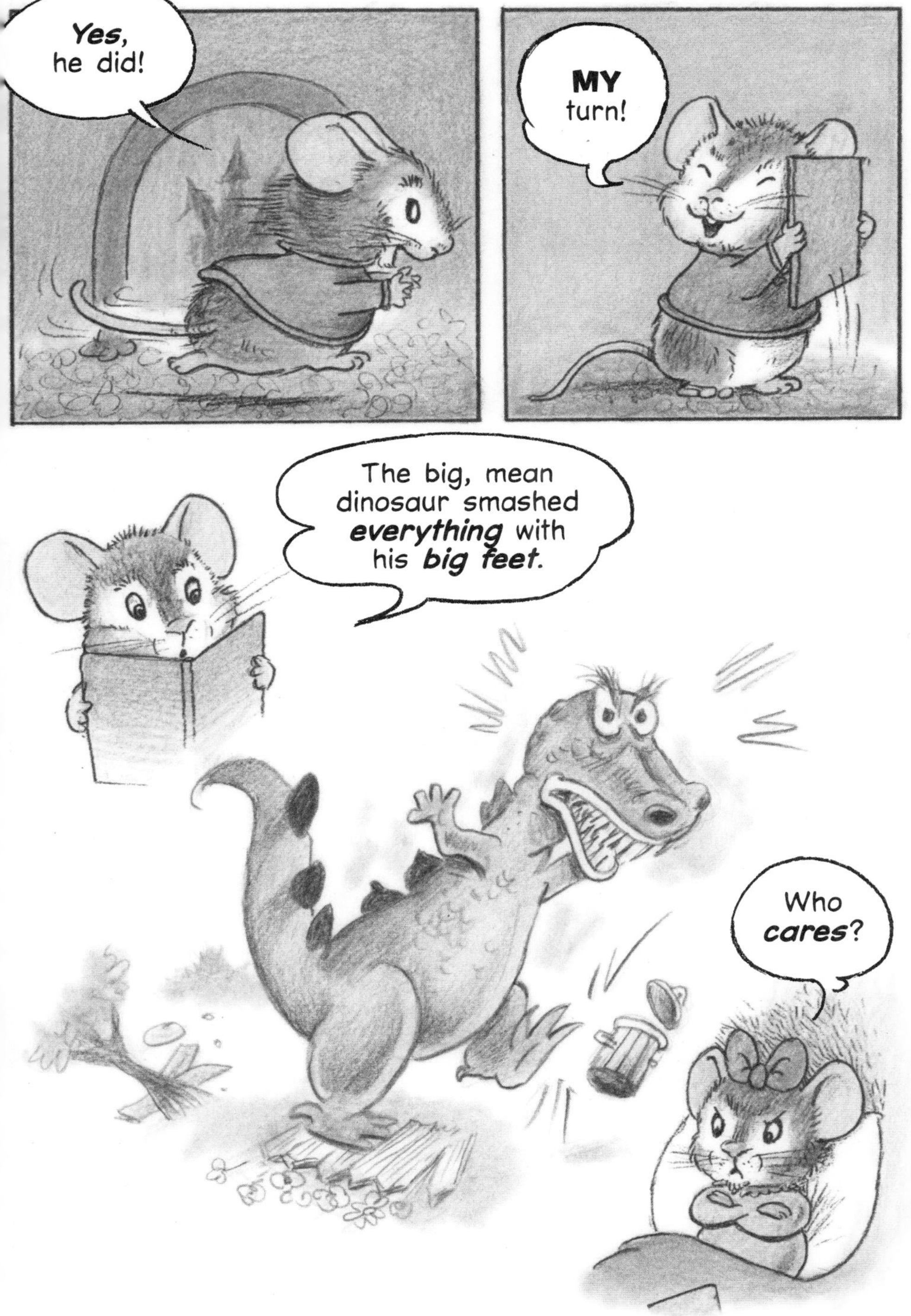
Yes, he did!
MY turn!
The big, mean dinosaur smashed ***everything*** with his ***big feet***.
Who ***cares***?

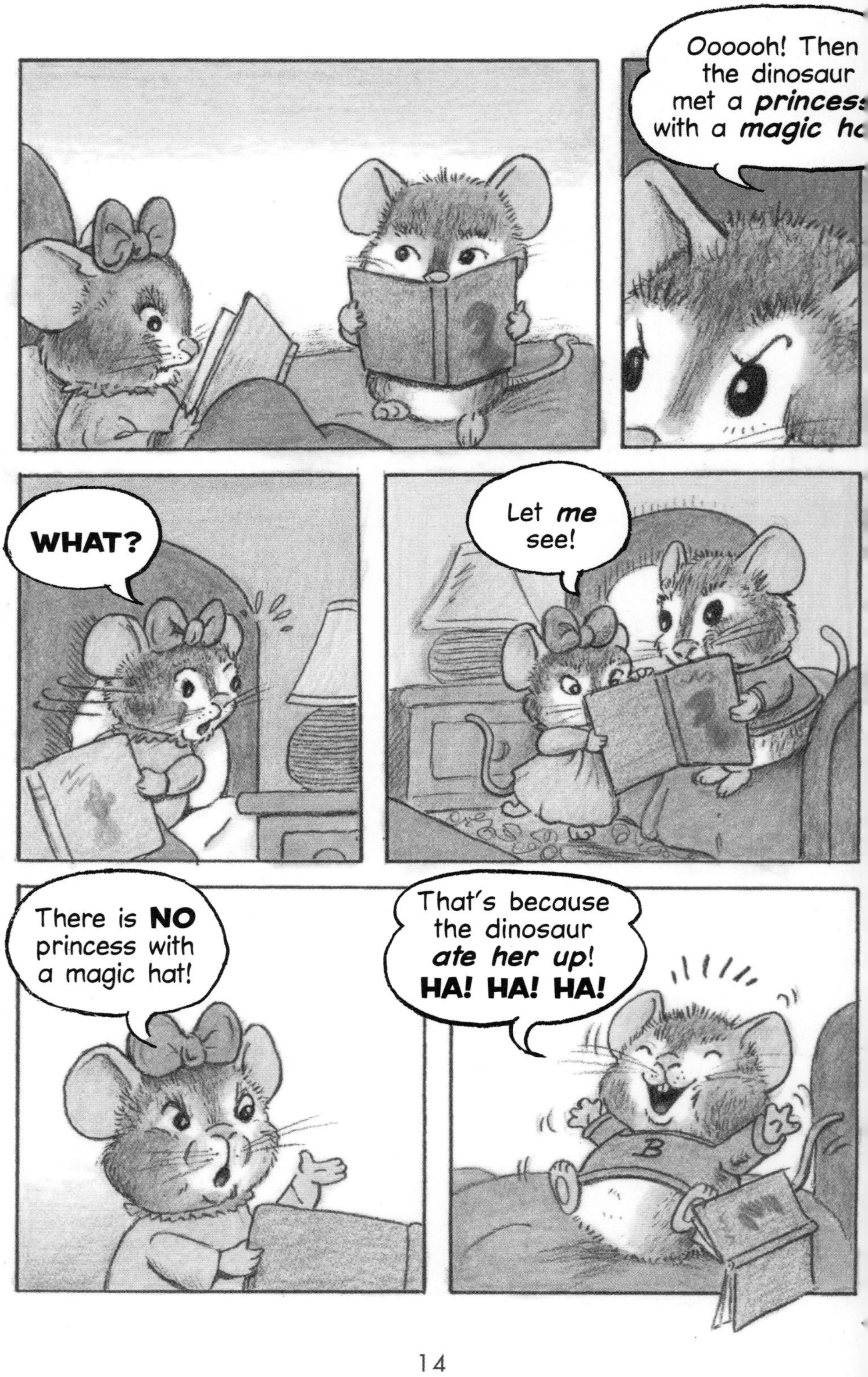
Oooooh! Then the dinosaur met a ***princes*** with a ***magic h***
WHAT?
Let ***me*** see!
There is **NO** princess with a magic hat!
That's because the dinosaur ***ate her up***! **HA! HA! HA!**

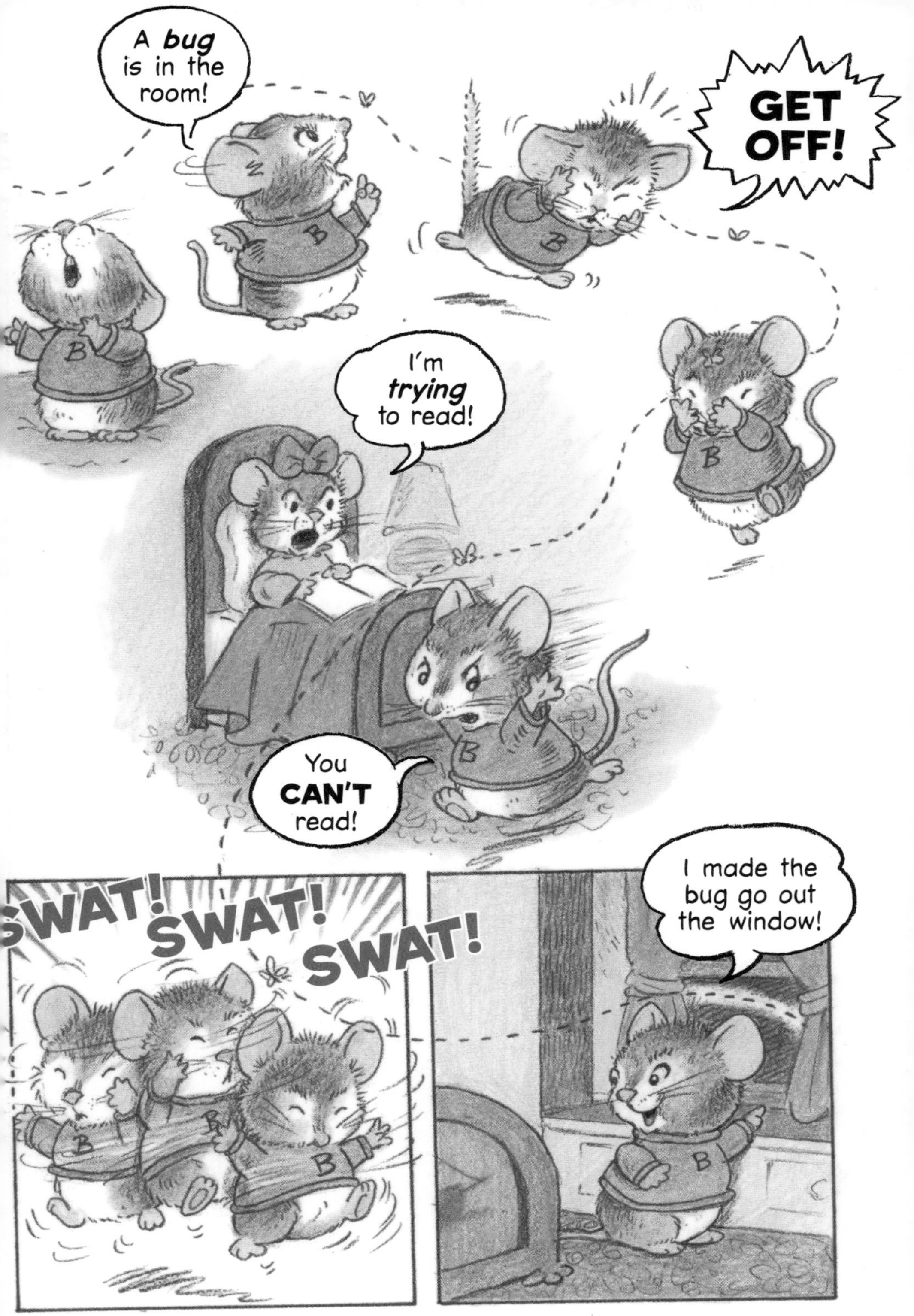
A *bug* is in the room!
GET OFF!
I'm *trying* to read!
You **CAN'T** read!
SWAT! SWAT! SWAT!
I made the bug go out the window!

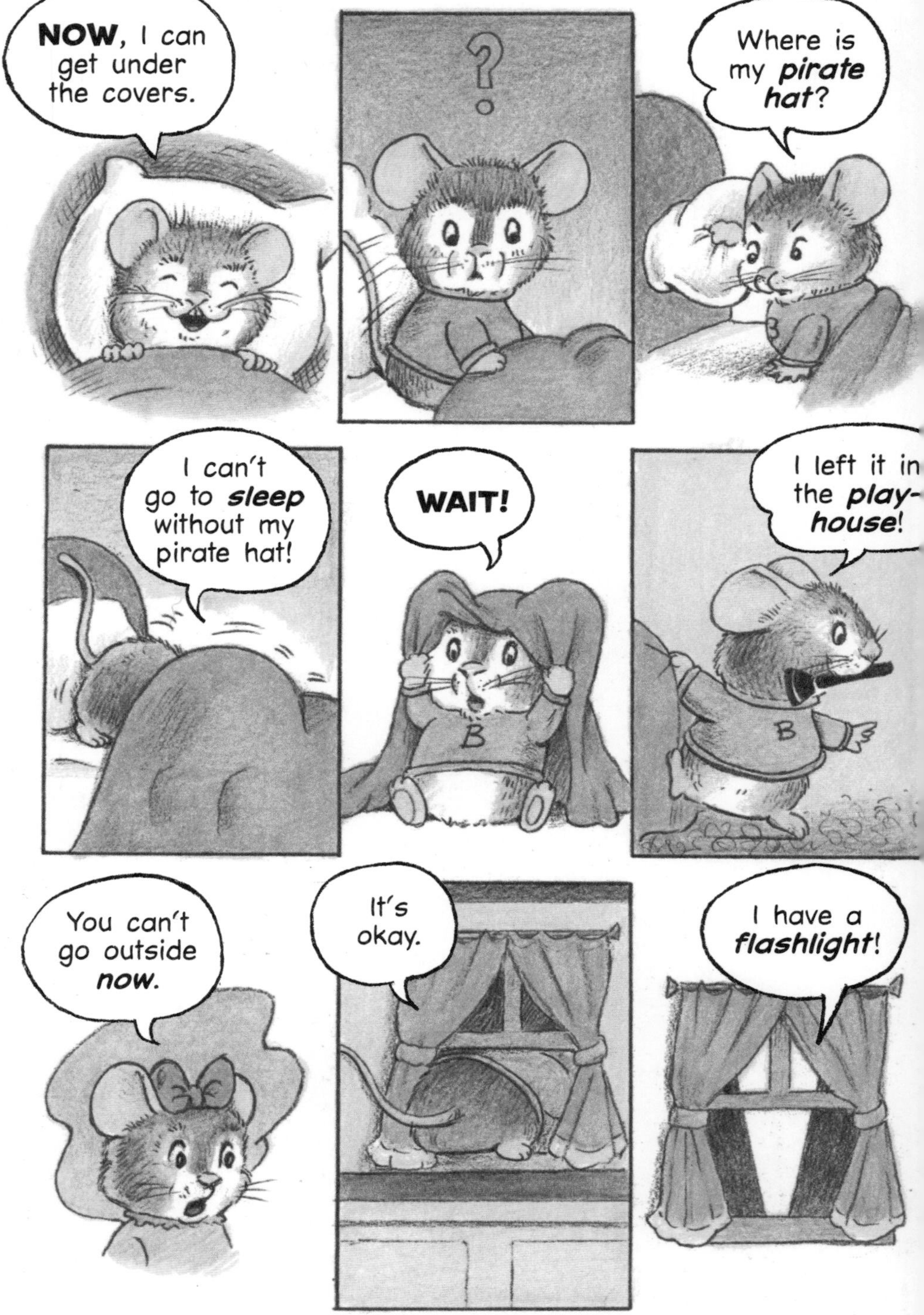
NOW, I can get under the covers.
?
Where is my pirate hat?
I can't go to sleep without my pirate hat!
WAIT!
I left it in the play-house!
You can't go outside now.
It's okay.
I have a flashlight!

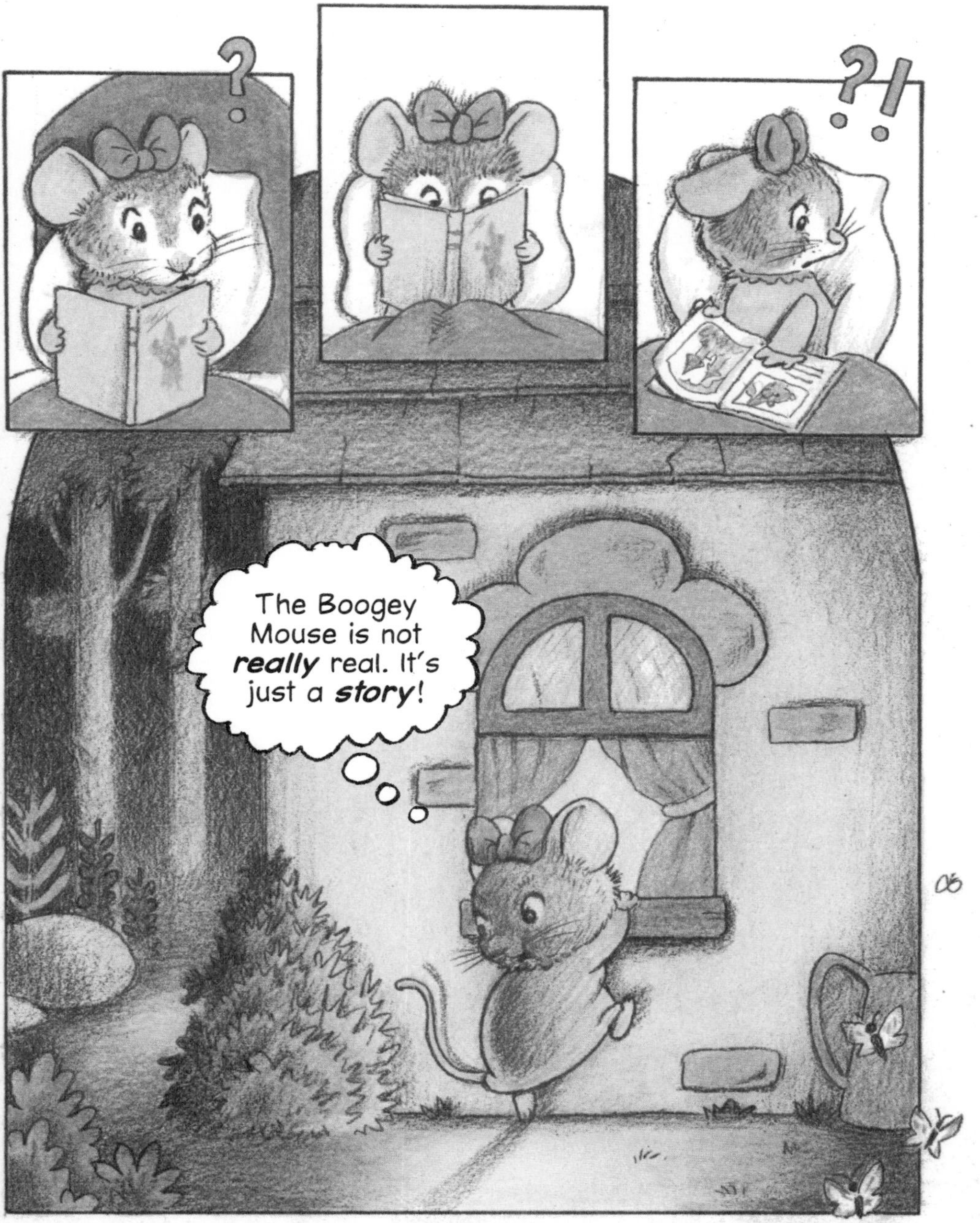
?
?!
The Boogey Mouse is not ***really*** real. It's just a ***story***!

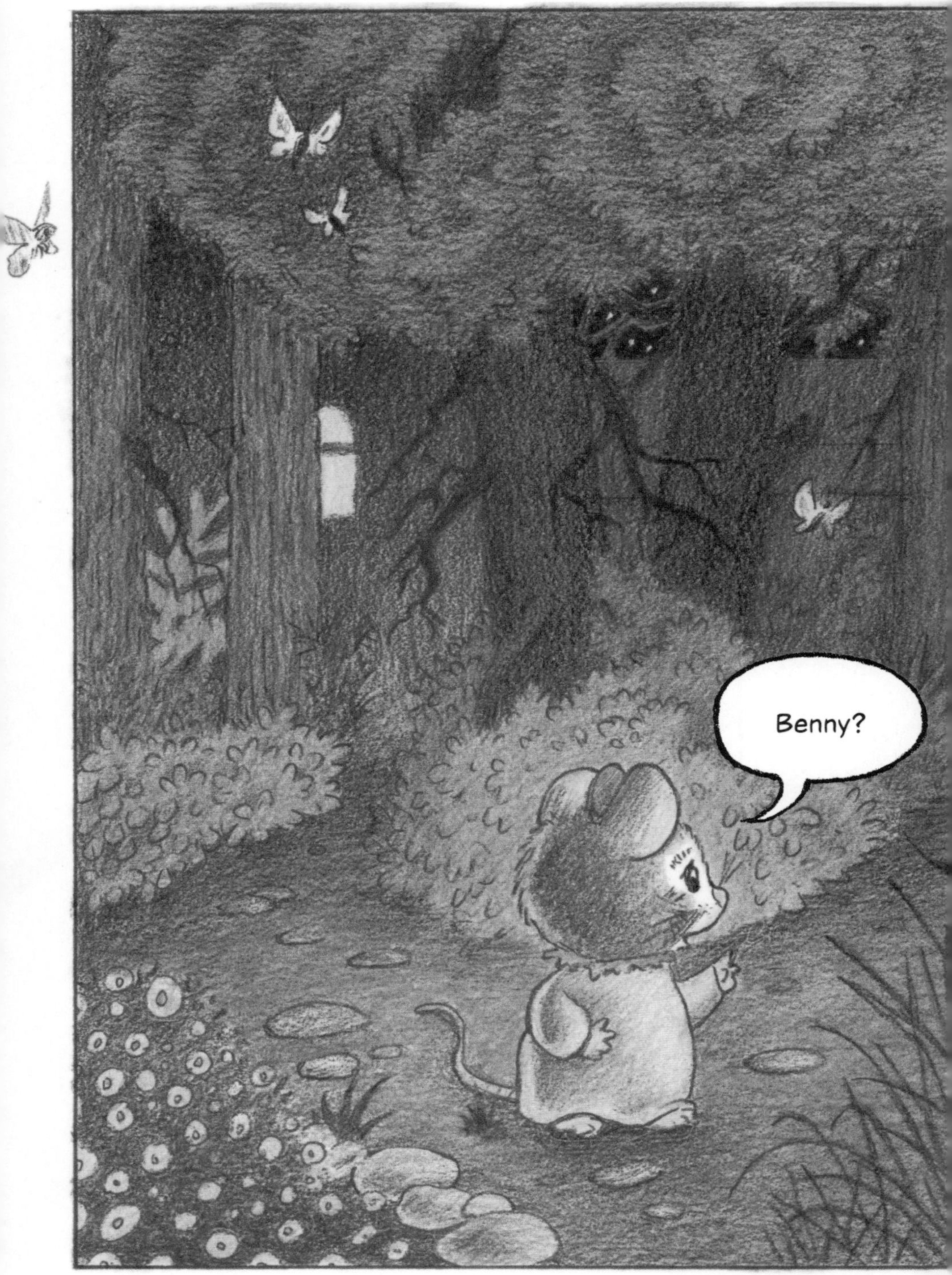
Benny?

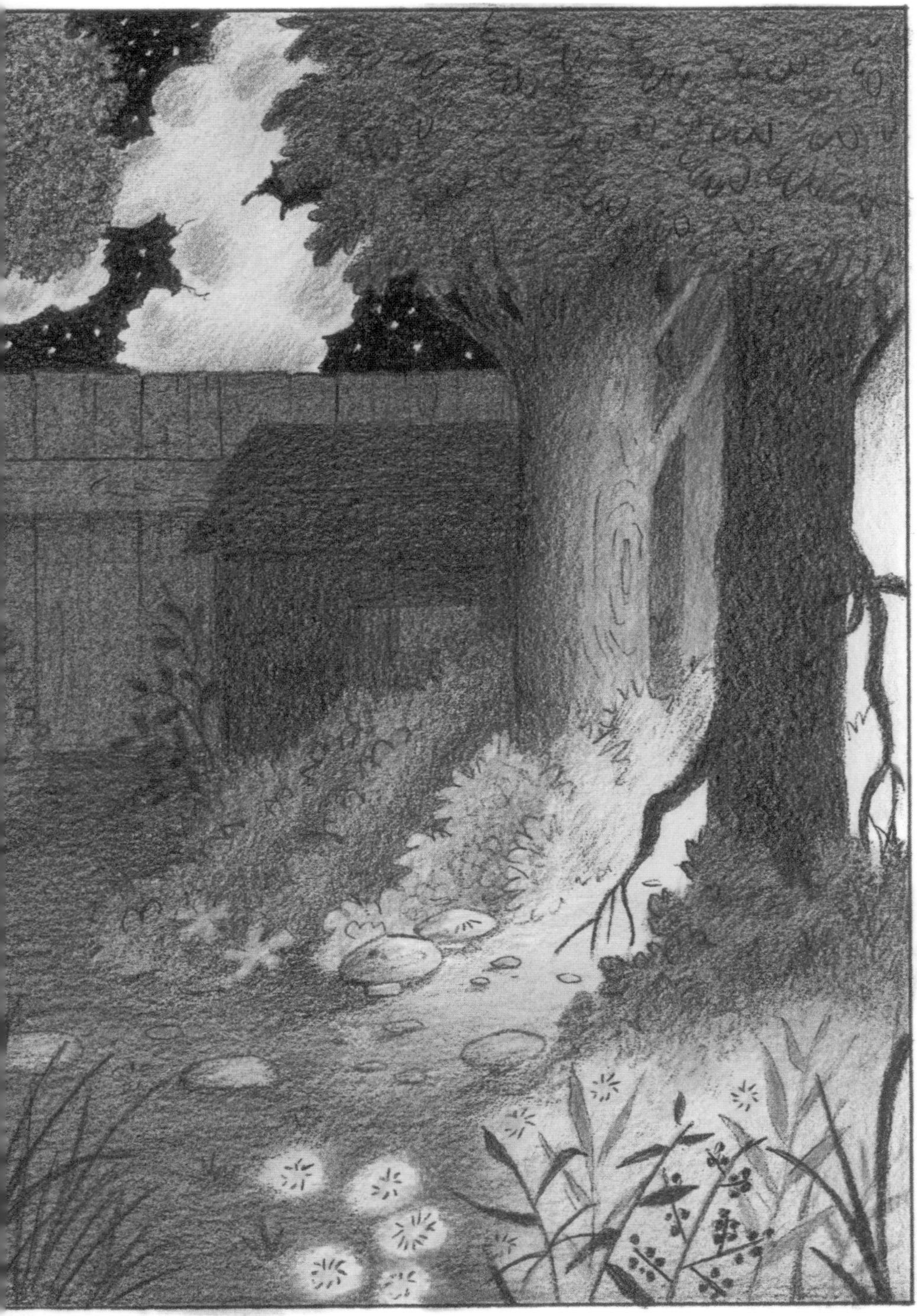

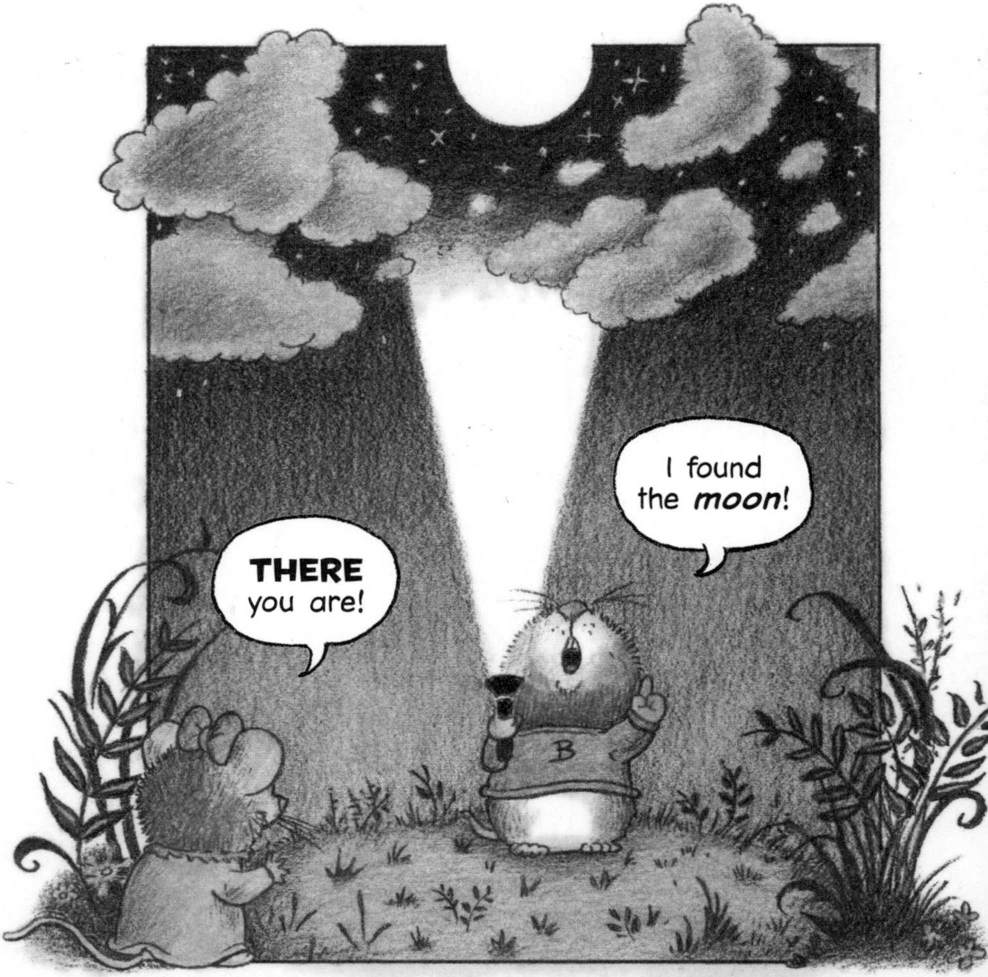
THERE you are!
I found the moon!

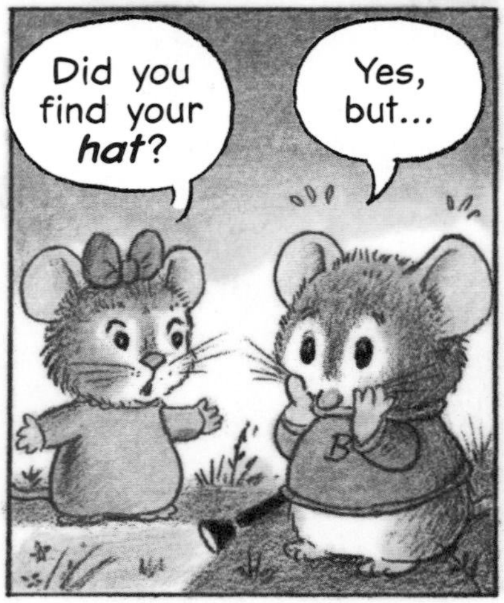
Did you find your hat?
Yes, but...

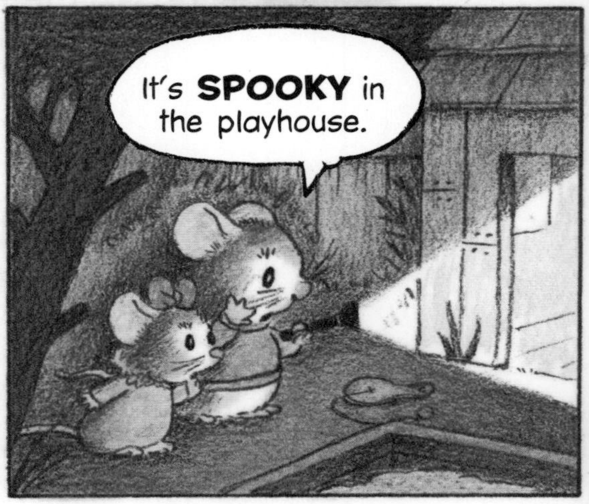
It's SPOOKY in the playhouse.

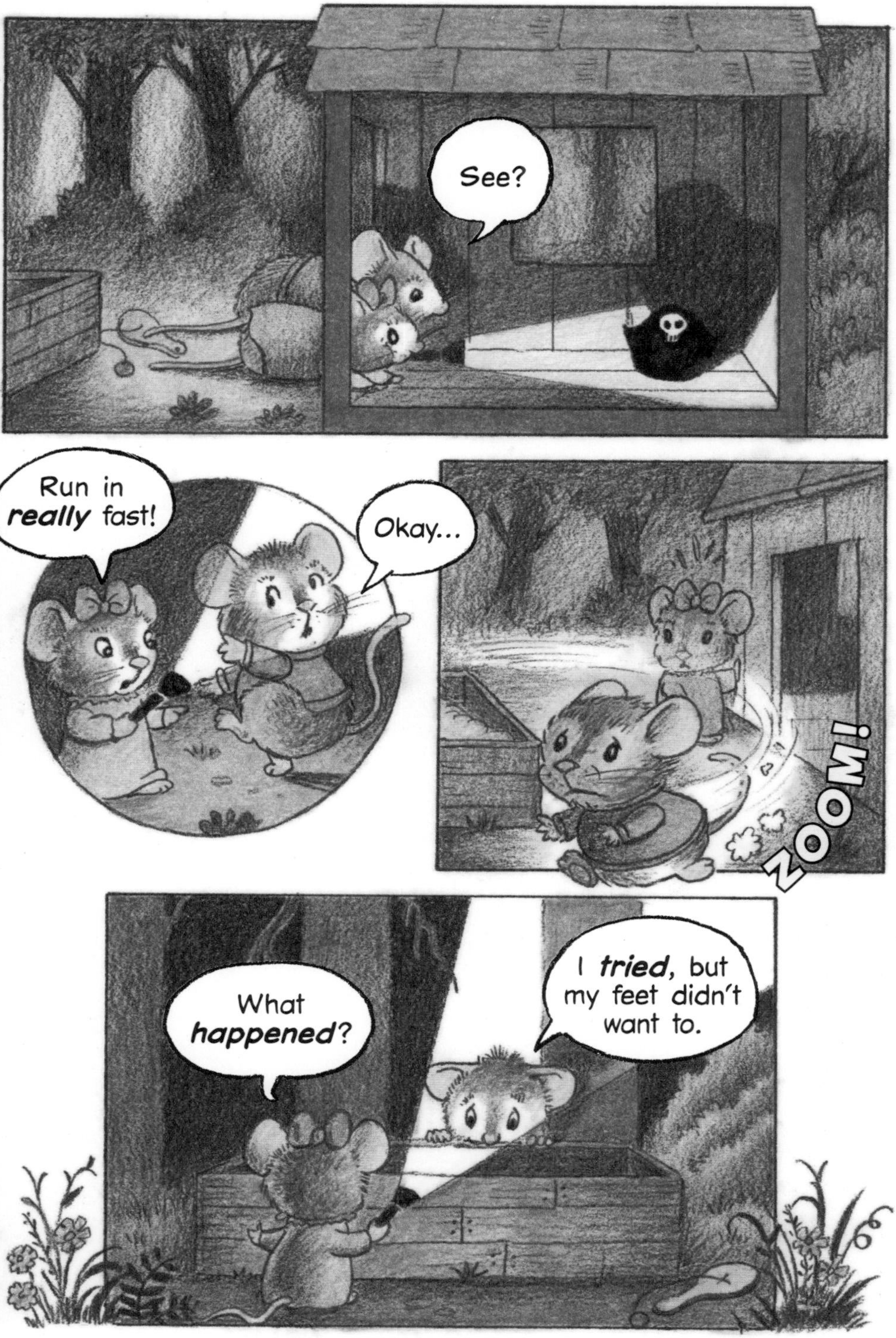
See?
Run in *really* fast!
Okay...
ZOOM!
What *happened*?
I *tried*, but my feet didn't want to.

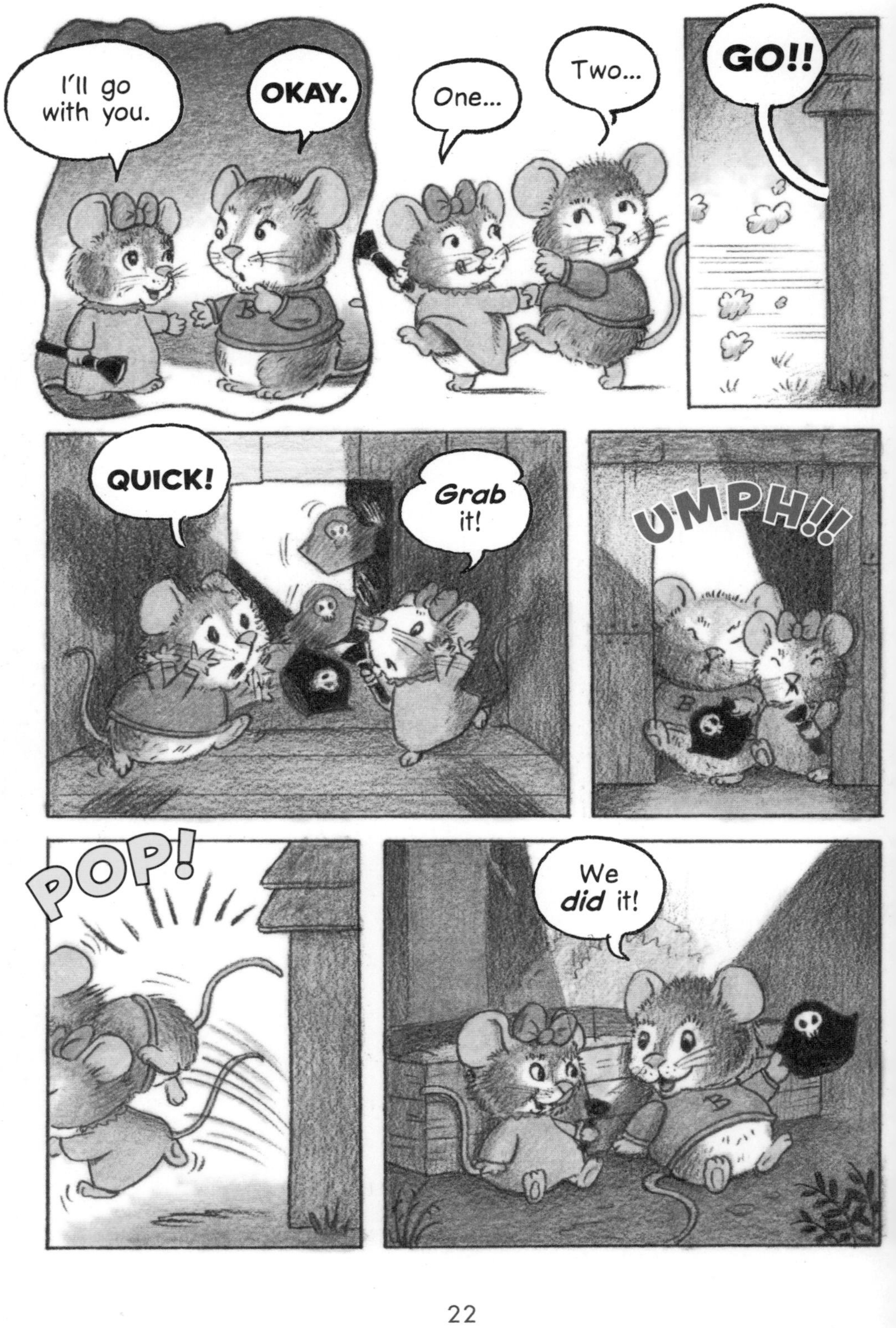
I'll go with you.
OKAY.
One...
Two...
GO!!
QUICK!
Grab it!
UMPH!!
POP!
We did it!

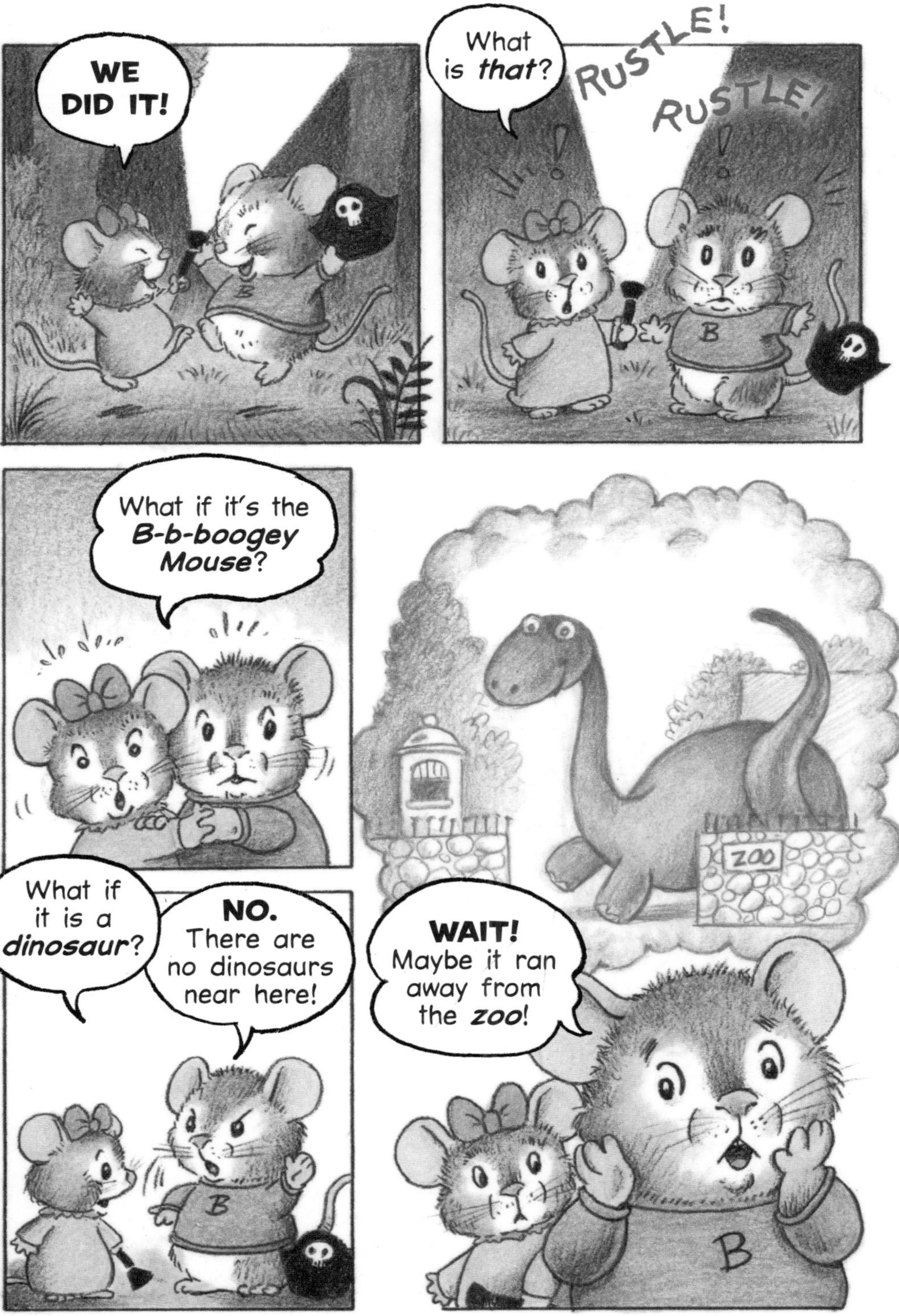
WE DID IT!
What is *that*?
RUSTLE!
RUSTLE!
What if it's the ***B-b-boogey Mouse***?
What if it is a ***dinosaur***?
NO. There are no dinosaurs near here!
WAIT! Maybe it ran away from the ***zoo***!
ZOO

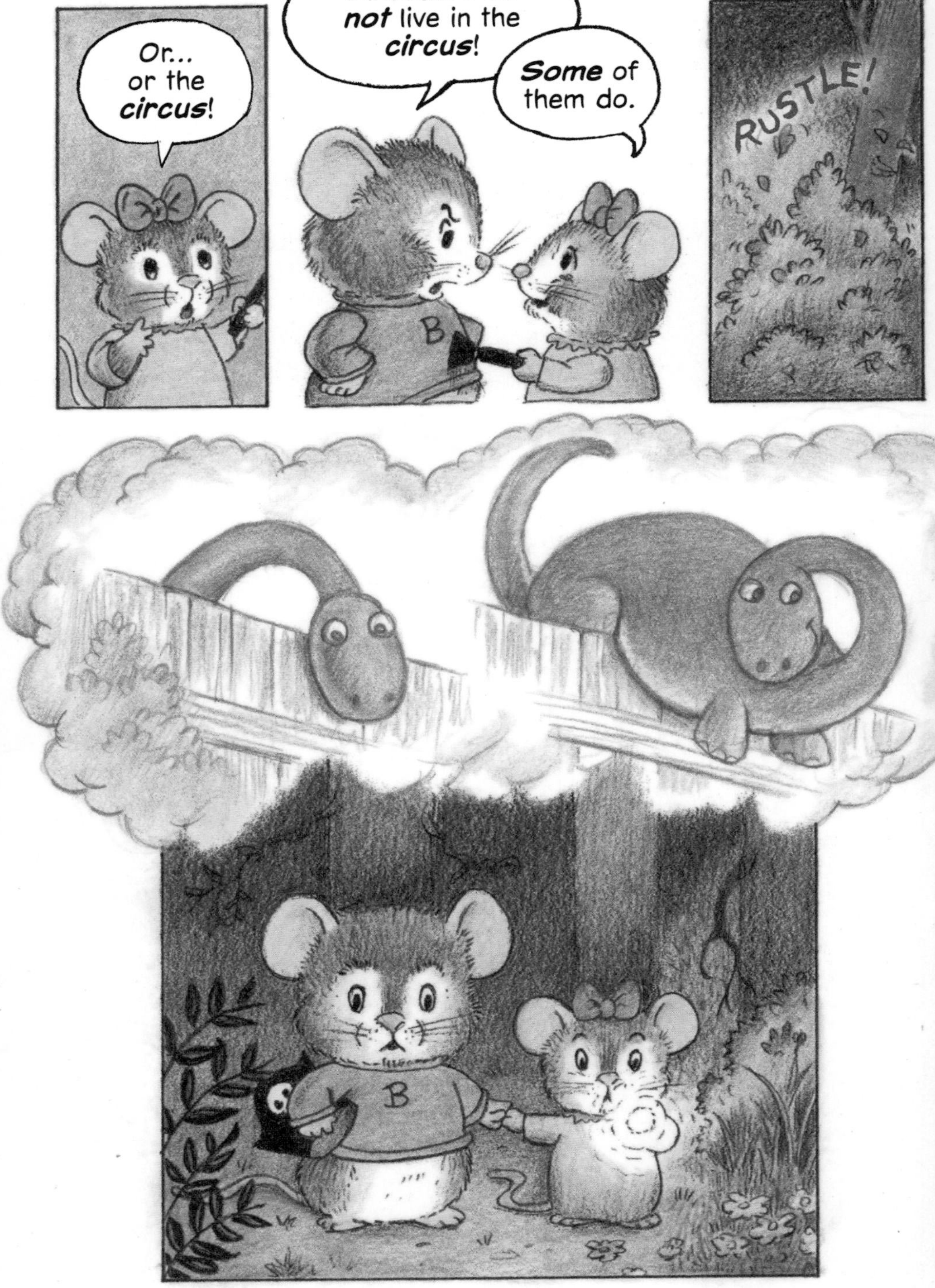
Or... or the **circus**!
Dinosaurs do **not** live in the **circus**!
Some of them do.
RUSTLE!

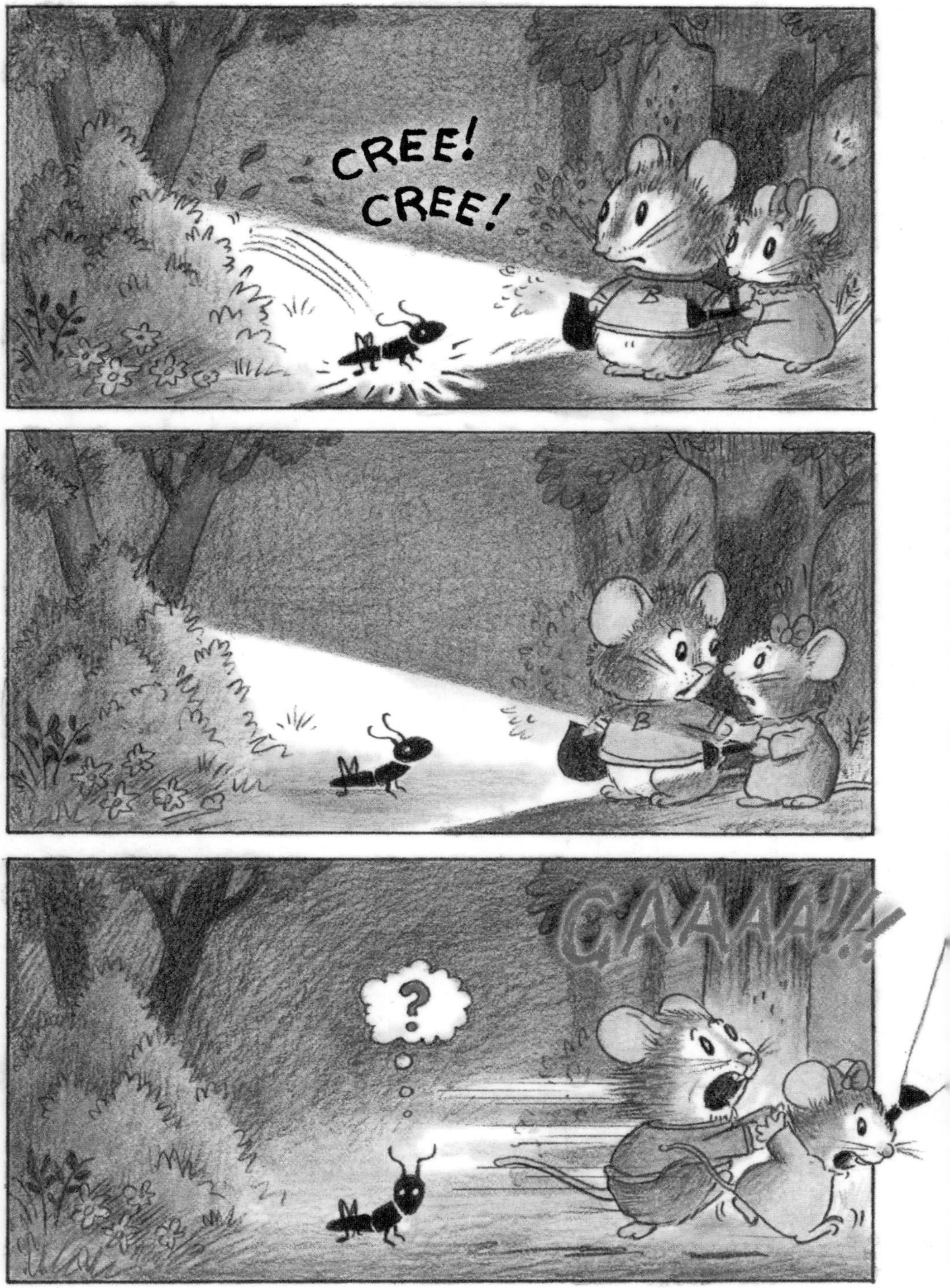
CREE!
CREE!
?
GAAAA!!!

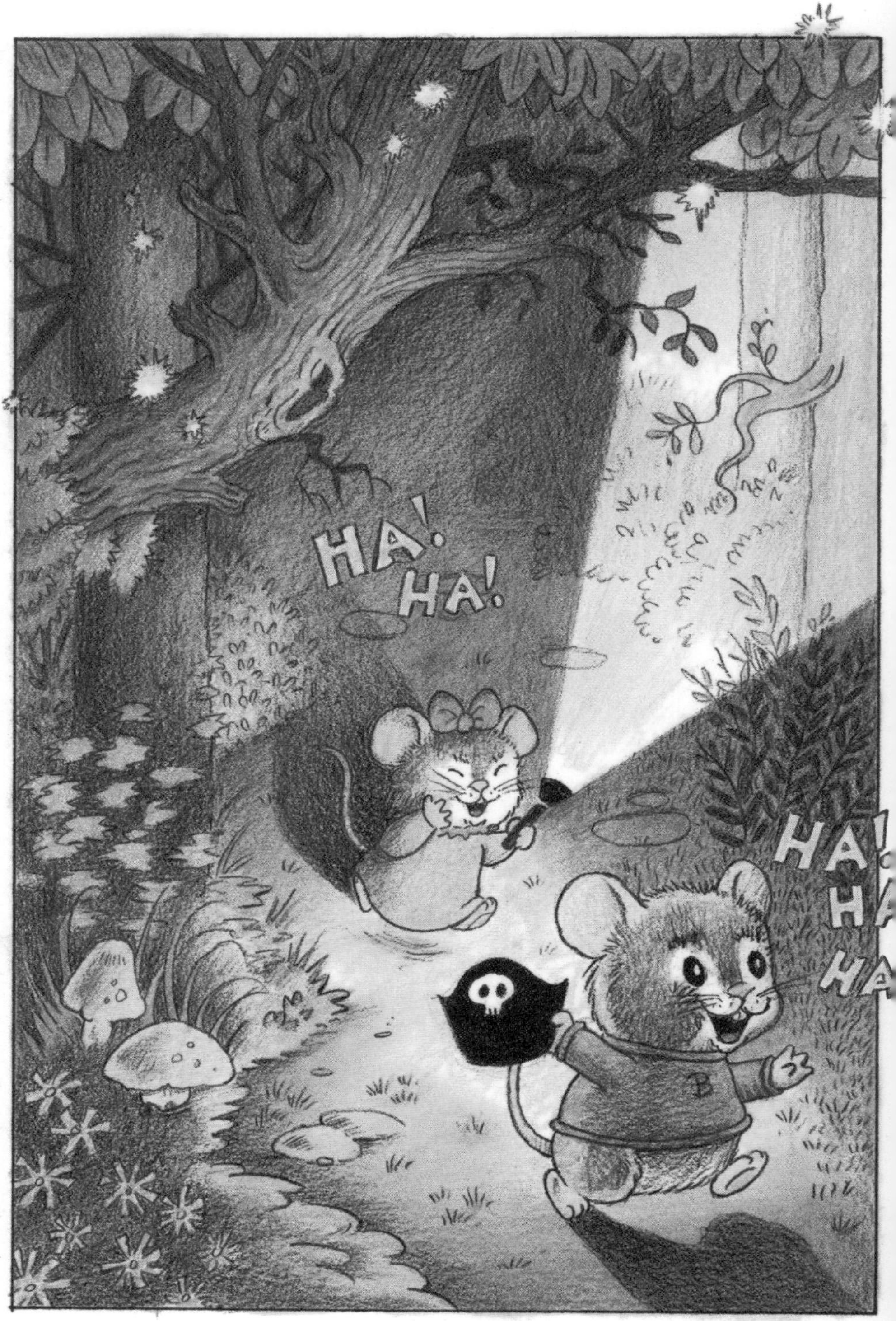
HA! HA!
HA!

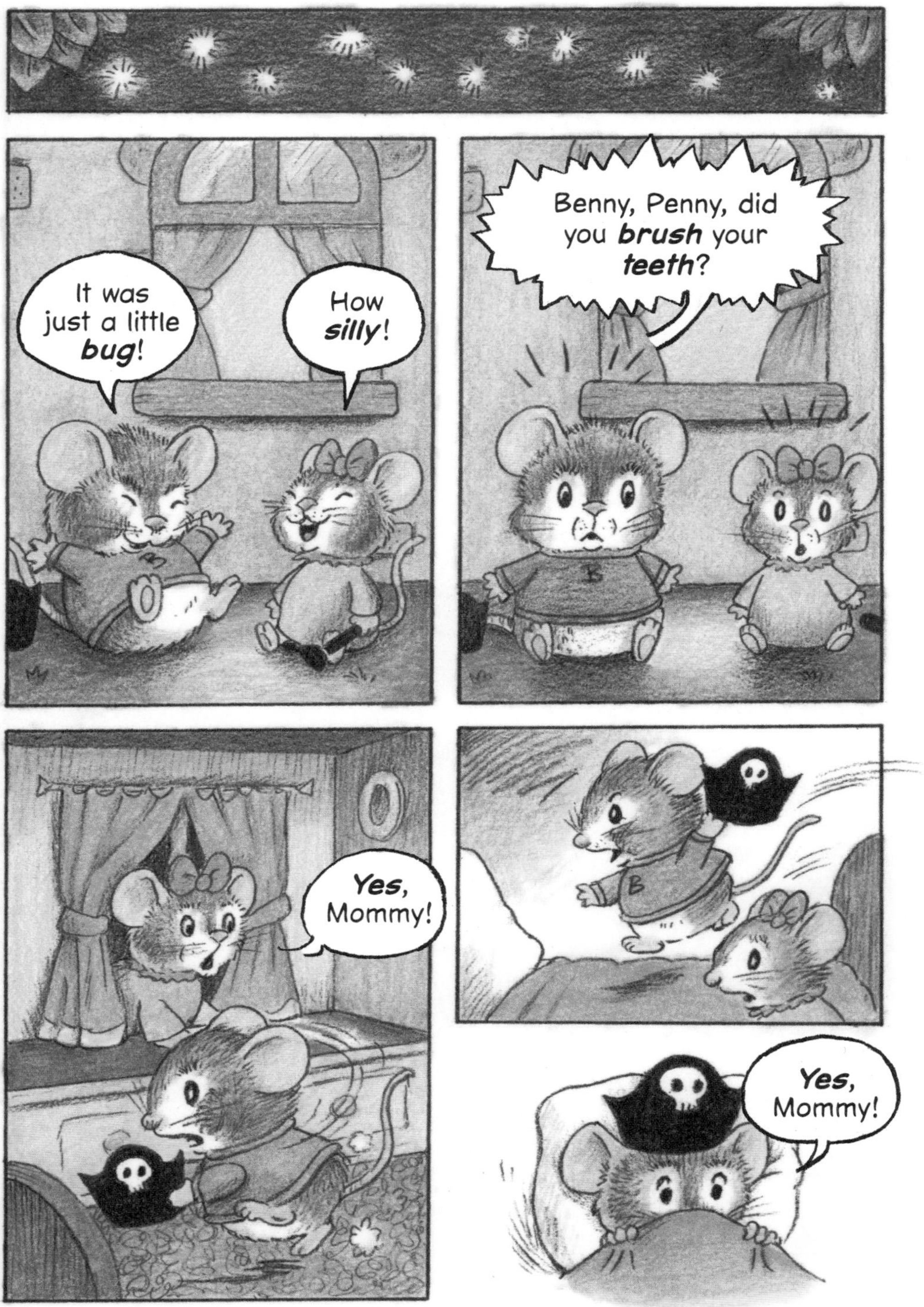
It was just a little **bug**!
How **silly**!
Benny, Penny, did you **brush** your **teeth**?
Yes, Mommy!
Yes, Mommy!

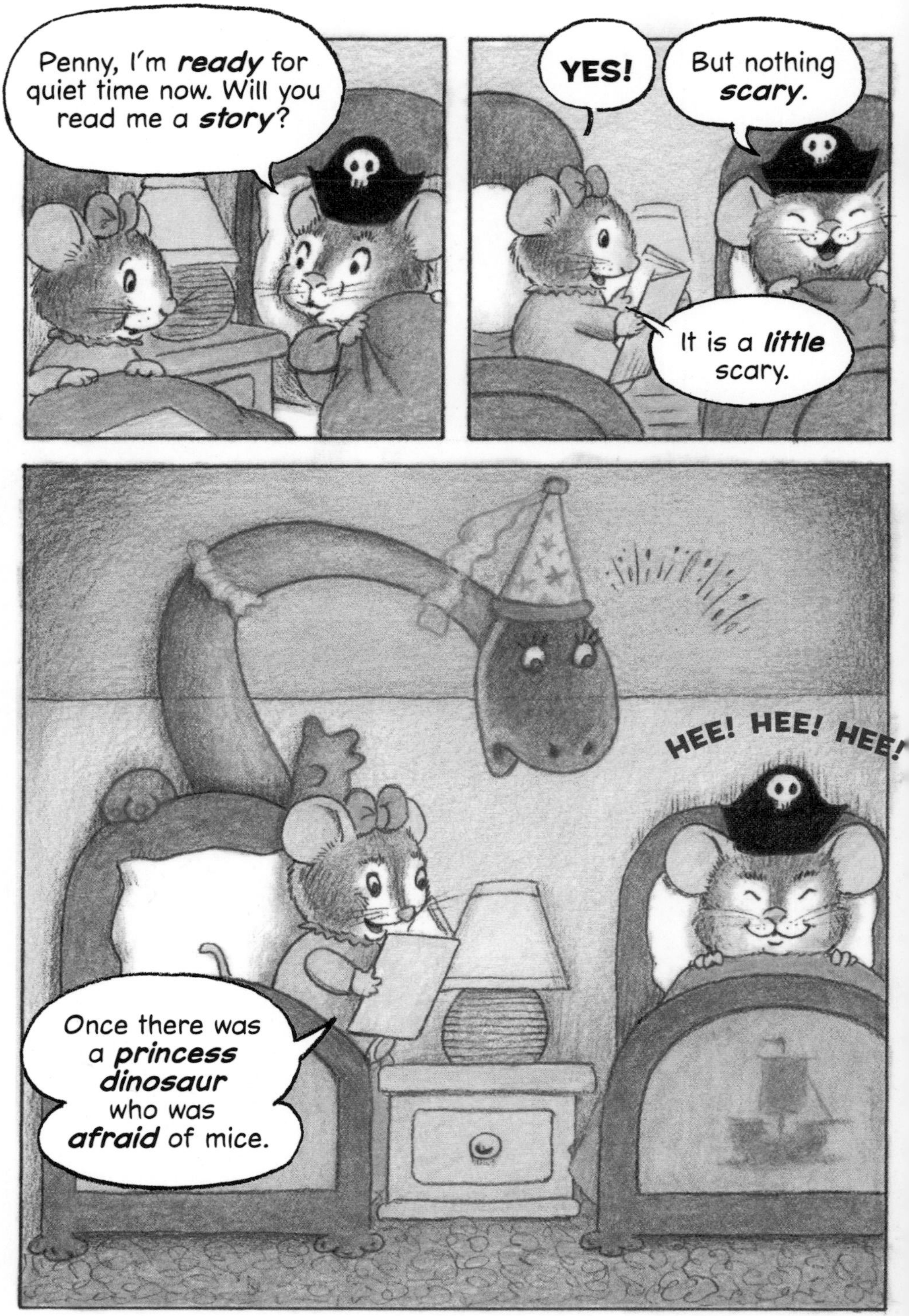
Penny, I'm ***ready*** for quiet time now. Will you read me a ***story***?
YES!
But nothing ***scary***.
It is a ***little*** scary.
HEE! HEE! HEE!
Once there was a ***princess dinosaur*** who was ***afraid*** of mice.

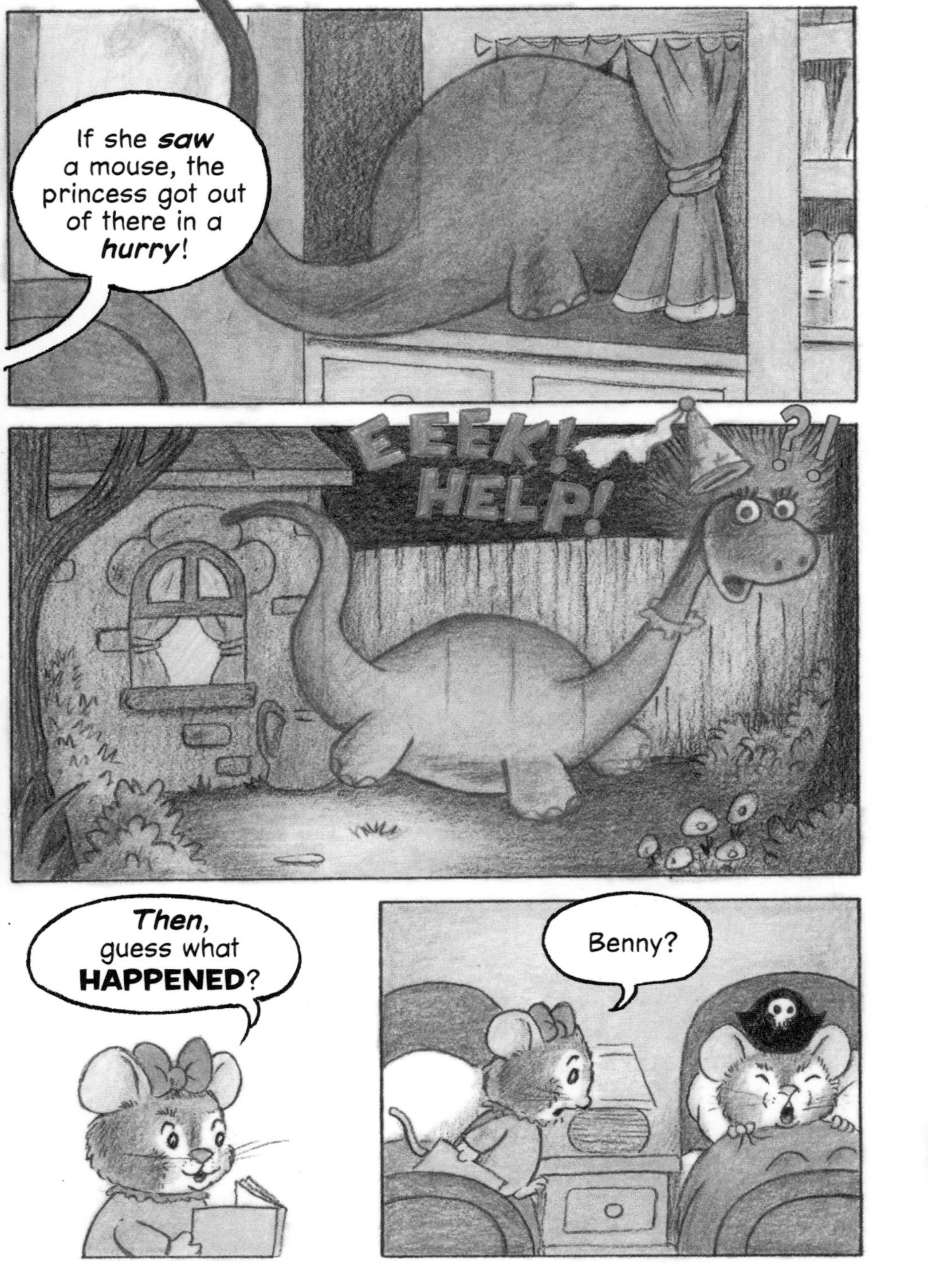
If she *saw* a mouse, the princess got out of there in a *hurry*!
EEEK! HELP!
?!
Then, guess what **HAPPENED**?
Benny?

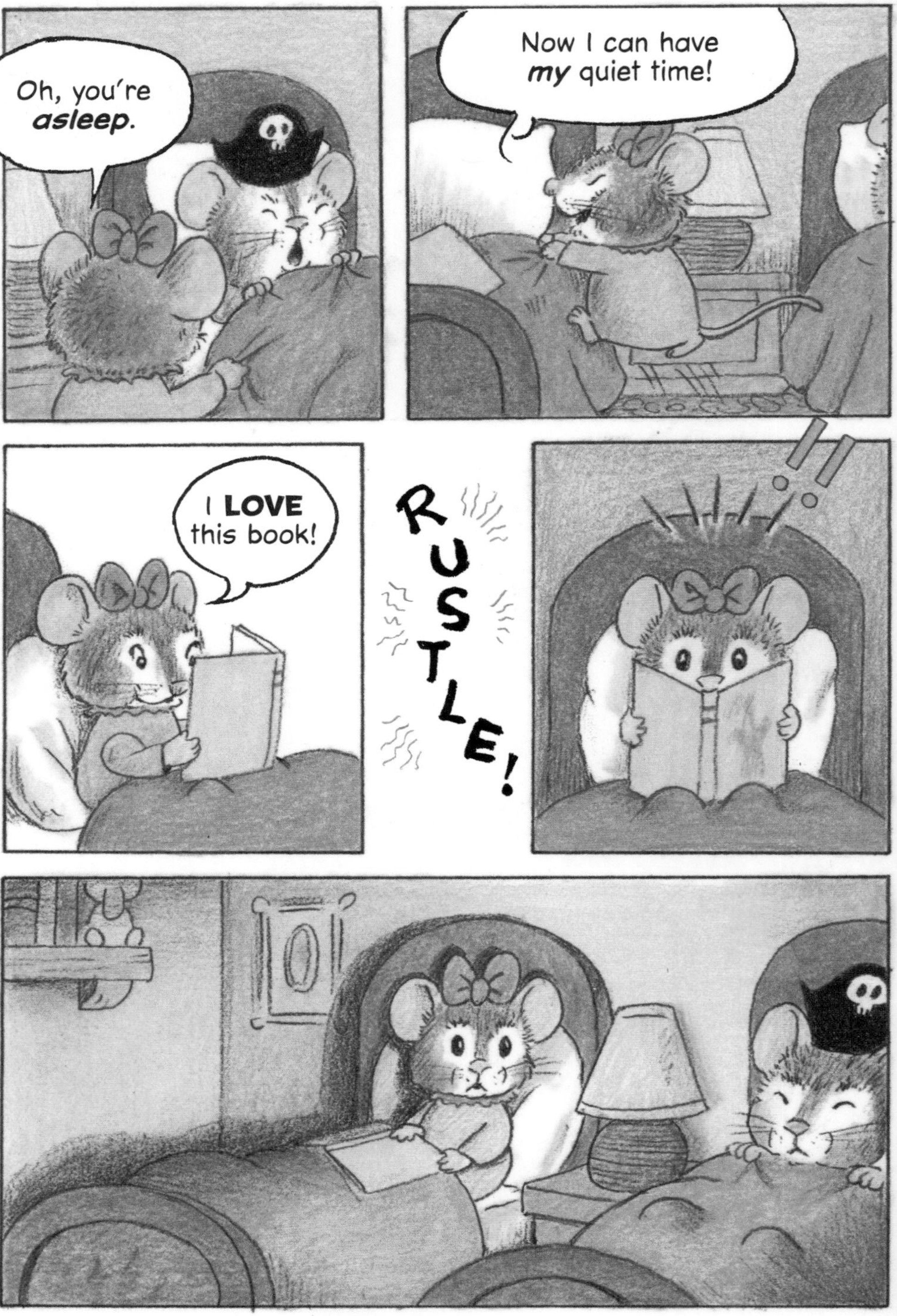
Oh, you're *asleep*.
Now I can have *my* quiet time!
I **LOVE** this book!
RUSTLE!
!!

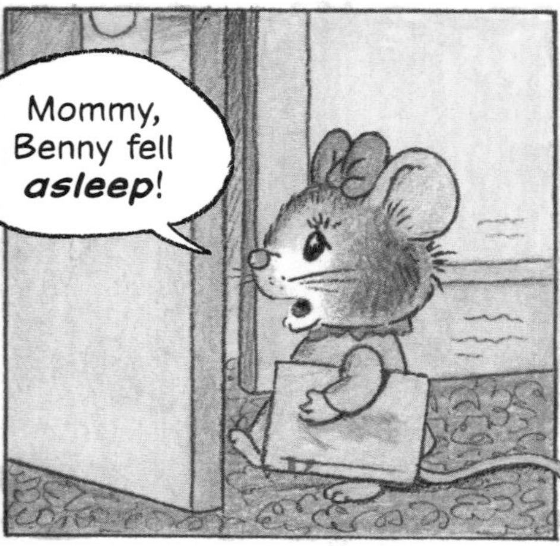
Mommy, Benny fell *asleep*!

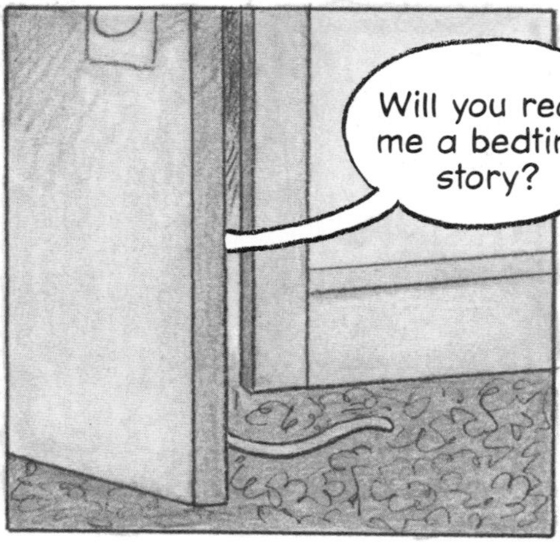
Will you read me a bedtime story?

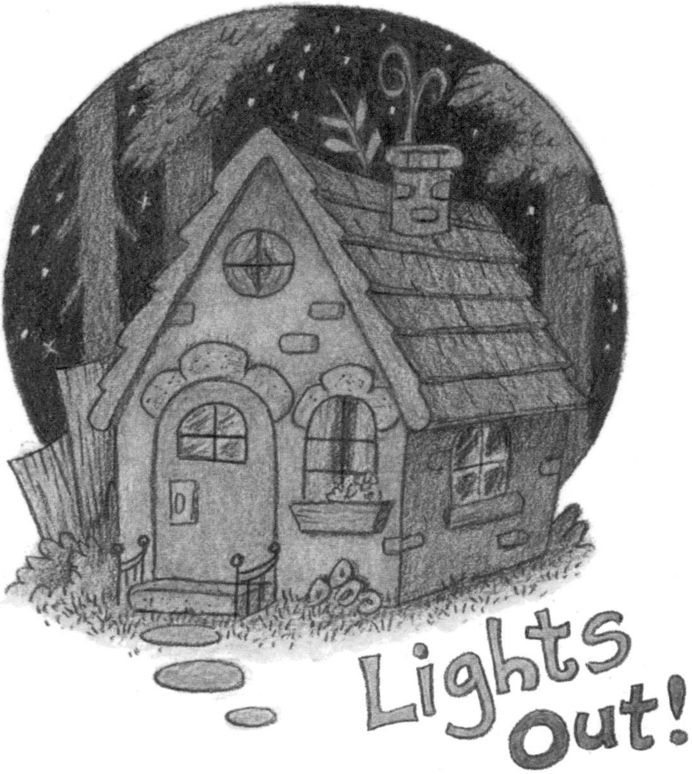
Lights Out!

ABOUT THE AUTHOR

GEOFFREY HAYES has written and illustrated over fifty children's books, including the extremely popular series of early readers *Otto and Uncle Tooth*, and *When the Wind Blew* by Caldecott Medal-winning author Margaret Wise Brown. He's beloved for his TOON Books – especially the Benny and Penny series, named "Best of Continuing Series" by Kirkus Reviews, and the Patrick Bear books. *Benny and Penny in The Big No-No!* received the 2010 Theodor Seuss Geisel award, an award given annually by the ALA's Association for Library Service to Children to the author of "the most distinguished American book for beginning readers." When Geoffrey was younger, his flashlight was his favorite toy.

Geoffrey says, "My flashlight had red, green and blue filters that could be turned to change the color of the light. I used it to put on puppet plays starring my stuffed animals."

HOW TO "TOON INTO READING"

in a few simple steps:

Our goal is to get kids reading—and we know kids LOVE comics. We publish award-winning early readers in comics form for elementary school, and present them in three levels.

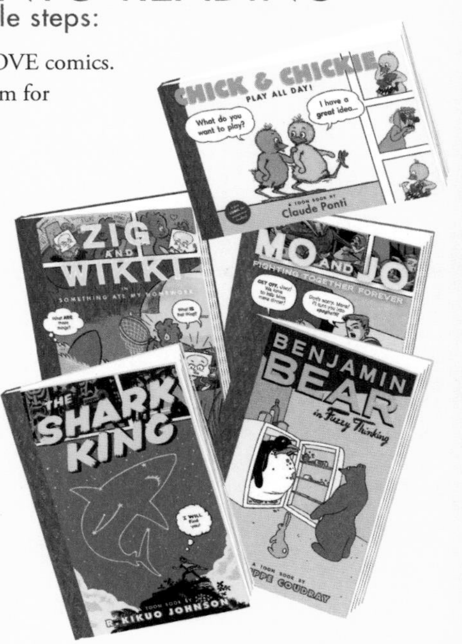
CHICK & CHICKIE
PLAY ALL DAY!
What do you want to play?
I have a great idea...
A TOON BOOK BY
Claude Ponti
ZIG AND WIKKI
MO AND JO
FIGHTING TOGETHER FOREVER
BENJAMIN BEAR
in Fuzzy Thinking
THE SHARK KING
KIKUO JOHNSON

① FIND THE RIGHT BOOK

Veteran teacher Cindy Rosado tells what makes a good book for beginning and struggling readers alike: "A vetted vocabulary, plenty of picture clues, repetition, and a clear and compelling story. Also, the book shouldn't be too easy—or the reader won't learn, but neither should it be too hard—or he or she may get discouraged."

The TOON INTO READING!™ program is designed for beginning readers and works wonders with reluctant readers.

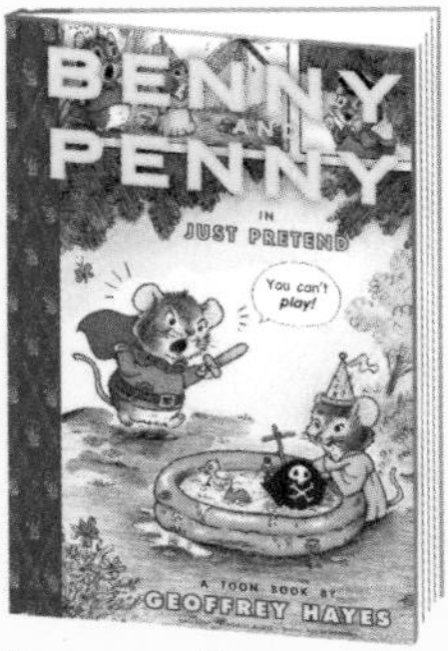
BENNY AND PENNY
IN
JUST PRETEND
You can't play!
A TOON BOOK BY
GEOFFREY HAYES

BENNY AND PENNY in Just Pretend

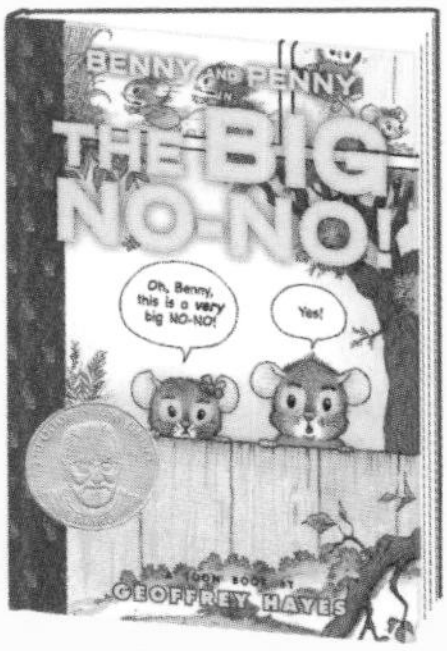
BENNY AND PENNY
THE BIG NO-NO!
Oh, Benny, this is a very big NO-NO!
Yes!
GEOFFREY HAYES

BENNY AND PENNY in The Big No-No!

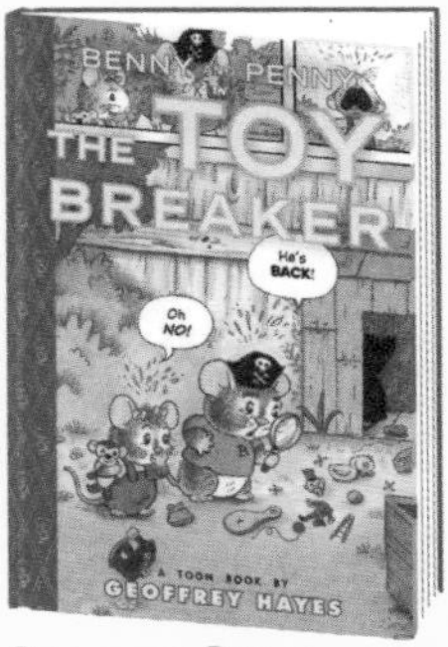
BENNY AND PENNY
THE TOY BREAKER
He's BACK!
Oh NO!
A TOON BOOK BY
GEOFFREY HAYES

BENNY AND PENNY in The Toy Breaker

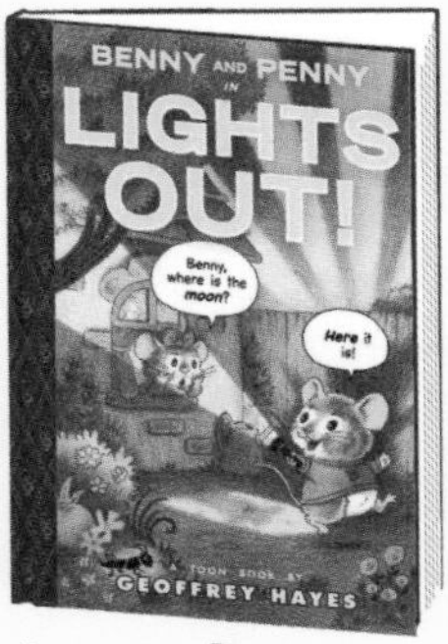
BENNY AND PENNY
IN
LIGHTS OUT!
Benny, where is the moon?
Here it is!
A TOON BOOK BY
GEOFFREY HAYES

BENNY AND PENNY in Lights Out!

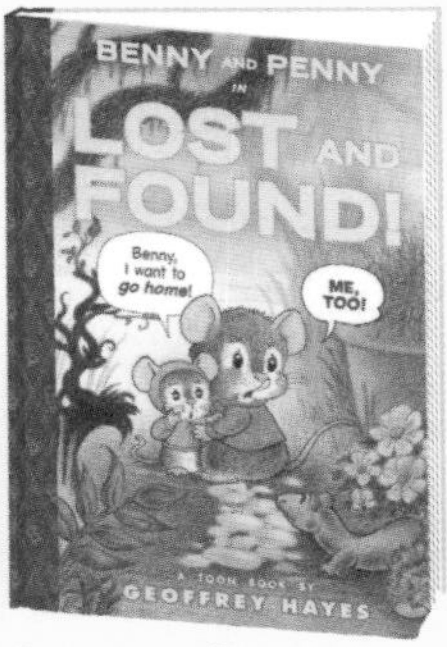
BENNY AND PENNY
IN
LOST AND FOUND!
Benny, I want to go home!
ME, TOO!
A TOON BOOK BY
GEOFFREY HAYES

BENNY AND PENNY in Lost and Found!

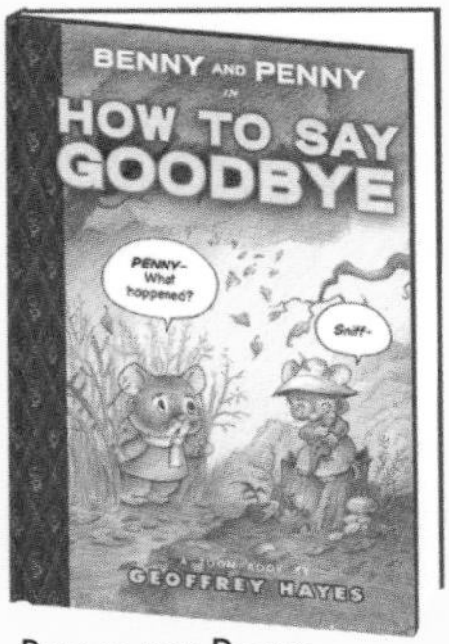
BENNY AND PENNY
IN
HOW TO SAY GOODBYE
PENNY- What happened?
Sniff-
A TOON BOOK BY
GEOFFREY HAYES

BENNY AND PENNY in How to Say Goodbye

Look for these other Benny & Penny books by Geoffrey Hayes

2 GUIDE YOUNG READERS

What works?

Keep your fingertip <u>below</u> the character who's speaking.

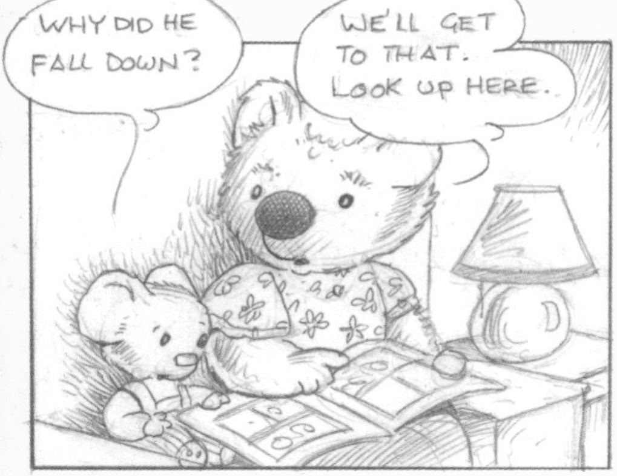
WHY DID HE FALL DOWN?
WE'LL GET TO THAT. LOOK UP HERE.

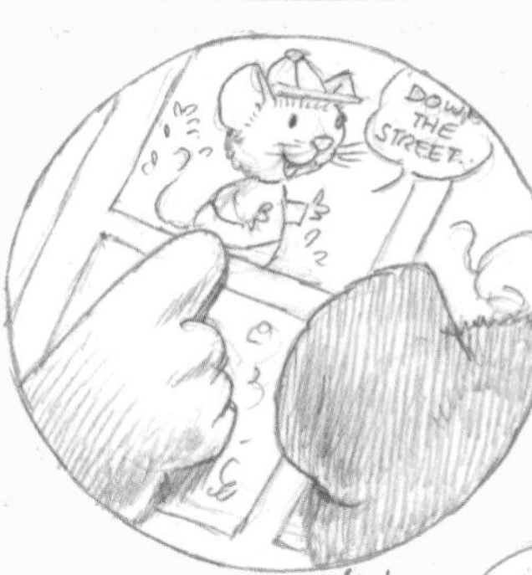
THE STREET.

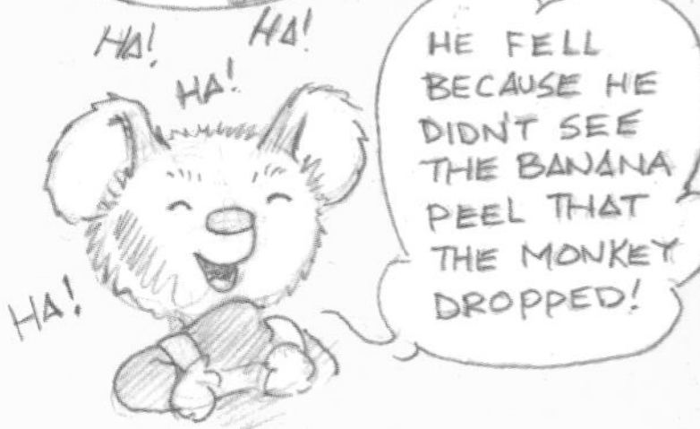
HA! HA! HA! HA!
HE FELL BECAUSE HE DIDN'T SEE THE BANANA PEEL THAT THE MONKEY DROPPED!

3 LET THE PICTURES TELL THE STORY

In a comic, you can often read the story even if you don't know all the words. Encourage young readers to tell you what's happening based on the facial expressions and body language.

4 GET OUT THE CRAYONS

Kids see the hand of the author in a comic and it makes them want to tell their own stories. Encourage them to talk, write and draw!

Get kids talking, and you'll be surprised at how perceptive they are about pictures.

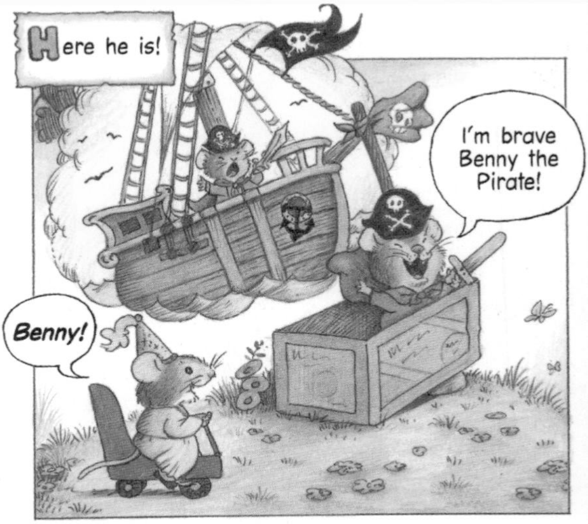
Here he is!
I'm brave Benny the Pirate!
Benny!

5 LET THEM GUESS

Comics provide a great deal of context for the words, so let young readers make informed guesses, and don't over-correct. In this panel, the artist shows a pirate ship, two pirate hats, and two pirate flags the first time the word "PIRATE" is introduced.